The Archives of Metaphysical Warfare

THE END IS THE BEGINNING IS THE END

C. Gaff

I dedicate this book to those most important in my life.
To God, with whom all things are possible.
To my children, all four of them. Without them I would not be who I am today. The biggest and most difficult journey in a person's life is to be a parent. Two of them gave me strength when sometimes I had none and always reminded me that I was loved. Without them it would not have been possible for me to make it through most of my life up to this point. The other two taught me that family is not defined by blood, it is defined by love. There is no greater adventure than parenthood. I love you guys.

This book is also for my sister, parents, grandparents, aunts, uncles, cousins...those who have tolerated my eccentricities over the course of my lifetime. They may not have understood my choices, but sometimes a person does not have to understand to give love. You are all amazing.

Honorable mention to the men, women, and creatures of MR. You know who you are, some of the best writers I ever met and the only place that I ever felt truly accepted. I would not be the person I am today without you all, I would not have had the strength to make it through some of the struggles in my life without your kind words and shoulders to cry on. Even though MR is no more, it will always remain my second home...a digital world where my many characters could come to life...there may even be a few of my familiar faces sprinkled in here and there. *Smile* Thank you for everything, guys.

Arachne sends her eternal love.

Last, but certainly not least, to my husband, without him and his support, I might never have finished anything. He is the light in my darkness, my sunshine through the clouds, his love guides me on our own journey. Even though not all fairy tales end happy, he will always be my 'happily ever after'.

Disclaimer From the Author: This novel is purely a work of fiction and not intended for any purpose other than to entertain. While some parts of it may be based on theology and history, this is not meant to portray any historical accuracy whatsoever. I did grow up within the church and have done a lot of research thereof, but much of the Biblical knowledge must be attributed to my husband who has a much more profound knowledge of the Bible than I could ever dream of having. It was through our many conversations that the Lord brought me back into his loving arms when I had been lost for so long. Even though this book is not the Word of God, it is purely fiction, it is also divinely inspired, because it was my returned belief that inspired me to write and finish this novel. I have written so many beginnings...but finally it was God that was able to bring me through to the end, just as it will be God that guides me as I continue with every book after this one. This is not intended to be blasphemous, prophetic, or even taken seriously. The characters within it, although some may have historical significance or references to individuals within pop culture, the character concepts are my own and not meant to be realistic portrayals or situations.

I am an artist, my words are my paintbrush, I would like to color your mind.

For those that are still with me, thank you and enjoy.

[**Side note from the author: In this book, you will find a different type of writing than most fictional based authors. They pause their stories or create an aside, some even force a person to do their own research, in order to explain things to their audience. This interrupts the imagination and takes away from the flow of the piece. These things bother me as a reader…

…so in the interest of those reading that may agree with me, I am going to give you both understanding and flow. There are multiple different languages within this piece, such as Latin and Hebrew. In the back of this book (and possibly in the books going forward) you will find translations and important notes from the author. These notes may also help readers to reference backward in future books. We will see how it goes. If my readers do not like this format, I may revert to a more traditional style in the future.]

The Archives of Metaphysical Warfare

Volume 1

When Hope had opened her eyes that morning, she could have never imagined the situation she'd be in. In fact, if someone would have told her that she'd be where she was, she probably would have told them to check their meds. However, here she was. In a fight she hadn't known existed, with a stranger who acted as if the world might be ending. Indulging him didn't make any sense. Her logical mind couldn't even comprehend her own actions.

Her life was fairly normal. It was mundane and routine, up until this point. She woke up. She showered. She dressed. She went to work. She came home to relax for a few hours. Then she went to bed. Day after day she repeated this cycle, in a mind-numbing haze. Sometimes she walked to and from work. Sometimes she rode the bus. Sometimes she caught a ride with a friend. The workday was, for the most part, the same as any other day. Except for a particular detail that had caught her attention almost immediately.

She remembered when she had first seen the stranger. She had watched him, as he stared out toward the empty night. At that point, his concern was not on her. It was directed toward the darkness, straining to see or hear anything that was moving. She hadn't truly been alarmed until he hurriedly walked up to her and grabbed her arm, pushing her in a different direction than she had been going.

The man directed his full attention to her for a moment, bringing a finger up to his lips in a shushing motion. He let go of her arm and signaled for her to follow. He seemed alarmed, as if something or someone dangerous was near. Her intuition urged her to trust him, though she had no idea why.

If it had been any other situation, she might have been attracted to him. He was not extremely tall, though taller than her by several inches. The man's frame was very thin, but fairly muscular for someone of his build. He had fair skin, as if he didn't frequently see a lot of sun. His hair was brown and cut at a shaggy chin length, and it was speckled with several strands of grey here and there. In the darkness, she hadn't been able to discern his eye color, though she assumed they were brown, as they almost looked black in the low light.

From behind, he seemed normal. He wore modern clothing and carried a backpack. After, what would have been, several city blocks worth of fast paced walking through the concrete ruins of the abandoned factory, a place which she'd been inexplicably drawn to; the two reached a vehicle, seeming to belong to her newfound companion.

He had protected her from the odd threat of whomever or whatever might have been after her. She hadn't seen anything, but deep down she knew that something was wrong within the structure she had wandered into on the walk home. She had been drawn to the area, but had no idea why, it was not on her normal route home. She also didn't know why someone might have wanted to hurt her. Who the Hell was *she?* Just a normal girl, with a normal life, with normal, everyday problems. She didn't consider herself overly beautiful, average and plain in her own eyes. Now she was sliding into the passenger seat of a shitty, old car, following a man who might have been a crazy person. She glanced around the car at the emptiness of it. There wasn't even trash on the floorboards or any sign of actual ownership. She glanced back to the unknown male who had taken the driver's seat. He placed his hands on the wheel, pausing to stare through the windshield toward the darkness once more. His right hand turned the keys in the ignition and the vehicle roared to life. They hadn't spoken since the moment he'd quite abruptly made his entrance into her life, saving her from what could have been certain death or could have been nothing except the rustling of a rabbit in the brush. For now, she wasn't sure if he was the hero or the villain of tonight's story, maybe a bit of both. This was the real world, not a fairy tale; it was very possible that she was in more danger inside of the car than she was out there. Her rational mind told her that this scenario was a bad decision, but there was a part of her that felt whatever the truth of the situation might be, it wasn't a scenario that was *normal* to what her version of the *real* world would suggest. The last few minutes circled in her mind, as she tried to gain a grasp of reality. Even though she hadn't seen anything, that didn't mean there hadn't been anything there. She'd had an odd feeling, a pit in her stomach, growing until it was about the size of a softball. That pit was why she had trusted him. The threat of a single man seemed much less than the threat of the unknown, for some reason.

The car ride was a silent one. The man was not much for small talk. He seemed so serious that it made her slightly on edge. She wanted to ask a million questions but thought better of it. She was still getting a feel for him. She tended to think that in most situations, she was an excellent judge of character, but that didn't always prove to be completely true. Sometimes her judgement was slightly off, tending to see the best in people while overlooking the bad, even if the bad far outweighed the good. It wasn't a terrible quality but tended to give her a bit of bad luck in life, so to speak. She wrestled with the concept over and over in her head as her eyes picked apart the state of the vehicle.

She reached forward and pushed the button for the glove compartment, which respectfully popped open. Nothing. Not even an owner's manual. Of course, this car was such an old model car, she doubted the manual to this specific POS even existed anymore. She slowly closed it back up and in doing so, felt eyes on her. She glanced toward the driver, who casually looked back forward again, a slight smirk forming over his facial features.

"Looking for something?" He asked, his tone suggesting that he already knew. He didn't watch her like so many people did when they held a conversation. Instead, he seemed to focus on anything else. The road, the dark landscape passing by in the headlights, the gages on the dash in front of him, all means to avoid glancing in her direction. She, on the other hand, had a hard time looking away.

"Not really," She replied, trying to be as collected as

possible. She wasn't sure whether to be nervous or excited, so somehow, she was an odd mixture of both. It wasn't long before they reached their apparent destination. The double wide trailer they stopped in front of seemed as if it had seen better days. The white paint that peeled off of the aluminum exterior, bubbled with rust and decay from decades of neglect and wear. Weeds rose up and tickled the sides, almost making whispering noises as they waved in the slight breeze. The only other noises out here, in the midst of the creepy looking forest that surrounded them, were the creatures that dwelled in the darkness. Tree frogs and crickets chirped creating the melody of a natural symphony that gave the night-time its mysterious allure. Owls made up the bass line and the creatures that preyed in the dark gave the shakes, rattles, and thuds of percussion. To an extent, it really was beautiful, even if what lurked in the darkness was often dangerous. Sometimes danger could be even more attractive than security. With that thought in mind, she glanced back toward where she expected the man to be, however he wasn't there any longer. Apparently, without pause he had left her behind favoring a direct path toward the trailer, leaving its door wide open behind him. She rolled her eyes and shook her head.

'Such genuine consideration.' She thought to herself, making her way toward the metal death-trap. The steps to the entrance groaned under her weight and she paused in the doorway assessing the inside of the trailer. It looked like a hoarder house. Possibly an organized hoarder, but just by glancing over the mess, a person couldn't tell one way or another. As she stepped inside, she noticed the dim light.

Shadows danced over the walls in the flicker of an old lantern, seeming to be the only light in the whole place. She put her hand to the light switch, flipping it on then off. Nothing, no electricity. She pulled her phone out of her pocket. The battery gauge read ten percent. It didn't look like she would have contact with the outside world much longer. She closed the door behind her as she wandered further into the maze of books and papers.

When she found him, he sat at a table, writing vigorously, as if his life depended on it. He was completely consumed with what he was doing, so much so that he didn't notice her coming toward him, until she was nearly right beside him. He jumped slightly, when he glanced up to see her standing there.

"By Jesus!" He took a deep breath for a moment, leaning back in his chair a bit, before sitting up straight once more. He didn't seem to mind that she was staring at what he'd written. It was beautiful, but in a language she couldn't read. She wasn't sure what it was, but it definitely was not English. He offered her a smug half grin.

"Do you read Florentine Italian?" It was obvious by his expression that the question was rhetorical. He placed his pen down on the book, leaning back again, now much more casually in his seat. He crossed his arms over his chest, looking her over now in the light, before making an inviting motion toward a chair across from him. The chair was covered in a thick layer of dust, seeming as if it had been quite some time since anyone had actually sat in it. She moved toward the chair, brushing it off before sitting down. She didn't bother to answer his question, as it didn't seem necessary. "I am sure you have questions, do you not?"

She shrugged her shoulders, continuing to glance around at all of the books and papers. Most looked fairly old, but some, much like the one in front of him, seemed newer. It was a hardbound book, though it didn't seem like there was anything special about it, it looked much like one of the diary style sketch books they sold in the Wal-Mart craft section. One thing all of the papers that lay about had in common, none of them were lined, notebook style. Some of them had rough sketches and what seemed to be notes. Something about them all seemed so familiar. She'd seen this style of sketches and notes before...somewhere. Of course, these were far from the same, but something about them was familiar.

"So...who exactly are you?" Hope asked, she didn't truly expect to get a straight answer. She expected some over the top, delusional, solidification of her belief that he was a complete loon. The answer he gave her was a bit of both.

"My name is Leonardo di ser Piero da Vinci. I was born in Florence, Italy, the fifteenth day of April in the year of our Lord fourteen-hundred and fifty-two." He stated this matter-of-factly, without even a glance away from her. As unbelievable as it sounded, it didn't seem like he was lying. He didn't flinch. He didn't fidget. He didn't pause. He behaved as if he hadn't just told her that he was a fifteenth century painter.

"So...Da Vinci, huh?" She questioned the man, giving him a sideways glance, while fiddling with some sort of tiny metal thing on the table. It was absolutely unbelievable, but she hadn't known what to expect in the first place, so she kept on with her line of questioning.

"Yes." Every time the man spoke, his odd accent came

through. He then went back to working on what he'd been doing, somewhat absentmindedly. She watched him closely, trying to get a better assessment of him. For some reason, she couldn't bring herself to automatically reject who he had identified himself as. Maybe it was her sense of adventure and imagination, maybe it was something else about him, she couldn't quite put her finger on why she couldn't dismiss him as a lunatic just yet.

"So, that would make you, what?" She paused trying to calculate in her head.

"Five-hundred, sixty-six years old. Would you like months and days, as well?" His answer was dry and a bit sarcastic, with almost a tone of annoyance. He didn't seem to like the personal questions, assuming she would have larger questions than that. He paused his writing long enough to answer, without looking up. His answer only perpetuated many more questions.   "Alright then. How is it that you have lived so long? I mean, the normal human lifespan was roughly under forty years old in the 16th century. How is it that you were able to survive so long?" She raised an eyebrow to him. Her questions held an air of superiority, as if she intended to trip him in, what the rational part of her mind believed to be, his lies.

"Healthy diet and exercise." Again, dry and sarcastic, though this time obviously very cynical and dismissive, in reaction to her haughty interrogation. He didn't seem to want to give her much by way of backstory or logical reasoning as to why she should believe that he was whom he said he was. He glanced up, then let out an impatient sigh. Reaching into his back pocket, he produced a wallet. From it, he pulled out a card and tossed it on the table. It was a state ID card. She picked it up and looked it over.

"This says Leo D. Jones." She looked from the picture on the ID to the man in front of her, then back again.

"I cannot tell them to put my real name on an identification card, now can I?" He once again paused, seeming irked with this specific line of questioning. "If I did that, they would likely toss me in the cage." He went back to writing, though he now glanced up occasionally, when he thought she wasn't looking.

"April 15th, 1983." She read off of the card. "That would make your respective age about thirty-seven years old." She shrugged lightly to herself, looking back toward him and for a brief moment his eyes caught hers, before he looked down again. "I suppose it doesn't seem far off in appearance." She couldn't remember specific dates without the help of Google, but some things seemed plausible in an oddly rational way.

"It is almost time for a new one, then." He reached forward picking up the ID, as she sat it down. He glanced at it for a moment, before sliding it back into his wallet, and returning it to his pocket.

He took a deep breath, staring down at what he'd written, one hand reaching up to scratch his head. This left a small amount of his hair sticking up, which made the girl want to giggle, but considering he didn't seem to mind either way, she just let it go. Once he was content with what he'd written, he closed the book, and slid it across the table haphazardly. He stood and walked halfway across the room before turning back to look at her. She could tell he was not accustomed to having company.

"Stay here." He said, before disappearing into the darker part of the trailer.

This was his only directive and so she waited. She waited for what seemed like forever. Though, without any way to judge how much time had actually passed, she had no way of knowing for sure. Without electricity, she couldn't charge her phone, and nothing seemed to be battery powered here either. She wondered how he survived without all of the conveniences that was normal in modern life. He did seem fairly acclimated to the English language and, to an extent, this time period, assuming this wasn't some sort of dream, nervous breakdown, or delusion, of course. She tapped her foot lightly on the floor to a song that played in her head. When she was sure she couldn't handle sitting there any-more, she stood. He'd told her to stay there, but what was he doing? He'd just disappeared into the back somewhere, doing who knows what, expecting her to sit there by herself all night? Maybe he'd forgotten that she was there. Maybe he was in trouble! After a few seconds of quiet deliberation, she decided that it was basic human decency to check on him. Even though it was very obvious that he could take care of himself, the pull of her curiosity fed her mind full of excuses to do the exact opposite of what he'd told her to do.

The hallway was dark, but because the lamp fed light in the previous room was not all that bright, it didn't take long for her eyes to adjust. More books, a few random contrap-tions, and pieces thereof lined the hallway. Moving further down, she still didn't see any signs of light or life. That was, until she reached a closed door. Beneath she could just barely make out the pale light of what was likely another lantern.

With all of the old books and papers here, he was lucky the whole trailer hadn't gone up in flames, the entire place was one big fire hazard. There was no answer after a few light knocks on the door. She had no idea what room was behind the door, but even if he wasn't in the room, it wasn't good to leave a lantern burning unattended. Again, another mental excuse, considering she'd just left a room with a lantern still burning.

She opened the door slowly and curiously. However, what she saw caught her off guard. Leaving the door ajar, she took an unconscious step backward, almost tripping on a rogue book laying there. She was unable to tear her eyes from the scene, but once her senses came back to her, she moved quickly back down the hallway. She found the seat she'd been sitting in and slid herself in it, racking her brain as she searched through scattered thoughts.

She wasn't sure how to handle this situation. She'd never had to deal with anything like this before, even in a normal scenario. She was freaking out. She pulled her phone out of her pocket, frantically trying to make it respond to her, even though it was very dead by now. Dead. Is that what she'd just seen? What exactly *had* she just seen? Her eyes were wide with panic, unsure of what she could do to help the man. Whether he was who he claimed to be or not, she wasn't about to just let him die. She balled up her fists and stood, making up her mind to at least try to do something. Even if she had to drag his lifeless body out to his car and get him to a hospital, she needed to do something. A lesser person might have taken off and never looked back, but somehow, she felt a sense of responsibility. Marching herself back to the room once more, she reluctantly looked toward his body, seeming to be a crumpled mass on the floor. She then glanced around the room to try to get an idea of what had exactly happened.

Her eyes darted around what once had likely been a bathroom, though apparently it hadn't been used as such in quite some time. Without running water, she supposed, there would be no reason to use a bathroom for its intended purpose. She went toward him, feeling for a pulse instinctively. She thought she'd felt one, but she wasn't completely sure, having only seen how to find a pulse on TV. Deciding to find out if he was just asleep, she tried to wake him by giving him a shake. No effect. It wasn't until she spotted the tiny bottle and syringe nearby that she felt the familiar uneasiness in her stomach grow, the unsettled feeling that had begun hours ago.

'Maybe he is diabetic?' She thought to herself, knowing that it wasn't likely the case. Not many insulin dependent diabetics were secretive about their medications. Besides, she seriously doubted this guy went to any type of medical professional. If he was who he said he was, then he was hundreds of years old, and he'd be a medical marvel. Science would want to study him, and the media would absolutely lose their minds, pasting his face on everything possible. If he wasn't, then he was delusional and would likely have been admitted to a psychiatric facility by now. She didn't have medical training, she didn't know what to do in this specific situation, and her phone was dead, so she couldn't call an ambulance. Her first instinct was to look at his eyes, to see what kind of state they were in. She figured his pupils, or the whites of his eyes would at least give her an idea of what had caused this. However, when she lifted his eyelids, she snapped her hand back. The action was quick, and she had been so startled that it caused her to lose her balance and fall backward, away from the man.

She had expected his eyes to be dilated or bloodshot or even rolled back in his head, what she'd actually seen made her heart pound in her chest and she couldn't stop staring at his closed eyelids. His eyes had been black, not overly dilated, not dark in color, solid black. The whites of his eyes had been non-existent. She tried to remember if she'd seen the whites of his eyes before. She had. She remembered, she had. In the dark, when they first met, she'd seen the whites of his eyes clearly, though not his eye color. Then once more, in the light of the lamp, she had confirmed that indeed he did have brown eyes. What had he taken that could cause that? To her knowledge, there wasn't *anything* that could cause something like that to happen. She picked the bottle up off of the floor, examining its contents. Only a drop of the clear liquid remained, holding it carefully and staying away from the syringe for fear of getting the unknown fluid on her skin.

He began to stir. Slowly at first, but he soon seemed to regain consciousness on his own. Hope kept holding onto the bottle and sitting beside him, as she watched him come to consciousness. He brought a hand up to his head, rubbing at it for a moment, as if he had a headache and it was within that moment that she noticed something that she hadn't when she'd been so concerned about him. The strands of grey that had streaked through his hair, were gone. It was almost like they had magically disappeared or possibly had never been there at all. Even his face somehow seemed younger, closer to the face of someone in their late twenties or early thirties, not the mid to late thirties he had seemed to be before. A confused look crossed over her face, and she wondered if it was just the lighting playing tricks on her eyes.

"I told you to stay out there." His voice was very direct and emotionless; however, it didn't seem to hold the annoyance it had before. He opened his eyes and looked toward her. She had to blink to make sure she was seeing correctly. His eyes were normal now, as they had been before. There was no trace of the black that had filled them only moments ago, making her wonder if she'd even seen it at all. He snatched the bottle from her and picked up the syringe that had remained on the floor, as he stood. Without another word, he slowly and unsteadily walked out of the room, leaving her there on the floor, questioning what she thought had happened. It wasn't long before she followed him back down the hallway. She found him once again sitting at the table, however this time he seemed to be looking for something in one of the books that had been sitting around instead of writing in the one he'd been working on before.

"What..." She paused, unsure how she wanted to word what she was about to say. The situation she'd just seen seemed as if it might be a delicate subject and one she never thought she'd need to have with anyone. On top of that, she wasn't exactly sure *what* she'd seen anyway. A part of her wondered if maybe she was the crazy one in this scenario. "What was that? What happened? Are you okay?"

Her barrage of questions was met with a very matter-of-fact stare, as if there were a completely logical explanation.

"What do you think you saw?" He met her reaction with a question. Whereas he wasn't sure *what* all she *had* seen, it seemed to be in his nature to question first and answer with only the amount of information that she needed to be satisfied.

"What was in that bottle? Was it some kind of drug? Is that why you think you are a 16th century painter?" She brought her hand up to her head trying to process everything.

"What it was, is not your concern. Though, to ease your mind...no, it was not a drug, per se..." He paused for a moment, before adding a small piece of information to his statement. "...at least not anything you could possibly be familiar with before now. Also, I am an entrepreneur, not simply a painter."

This made her more confused. Not her concern? She'd just found him on his 'bathroom' floor, and it wasn't her concern? Though, she did suppose that this *was* his house, and she really didn't know him. It was in that moment that she started wondering why she even cared so much. She didn't know this guy. He didn't know her. For all intents and purposes, he had basically kidnapped her, and he seemed fine now. She furrowed her brow and her expression completely changed.

"So when do you intend on taking me home?" She

asked, trying to be very direct and almost demanding, however in her voice it didn't quite come out as forceful as she would have liked.

"I do not." The answer was quick and simple. He didn't even look up from what he was reading.

"What?!" Her voice came out louder than she had intended for it to, it wasn't as if she was going to bother the neighbors, as the nearest person was likely miles away, judging by the woods around them. She wasn't an imposing girl. She stood at five foot, four inches and her weight, though well proportioned, was fairly average for a woman of her build. She puffed up, slamming her hands on her hips, just above the hemline of her jeans. "Do you expect me to walk home? You can't just keep me here! You don't even know me!" These loud statements gave birth to more and more pessimistic thoughts, as she remembered the many movie scenarios, she'd seen of being trapped in a cabin in the woods. "You're not going to do unspeakable things to me, are you? I promise you; I don't taste very good. I eat a lot of junk food and…" Her mind tried to think of the worst thing that she could possibly taste like and spouted out the first thing that came to her. "…dirt. Yeah, dirt. I have Pica. I love eating dirt." She was nervously rambling.

Calmly the man looked up toward her and gave her a look that made her feel like he was starting to think that *she* was crazy. He closed the book that was in front of him, placing his hands on it and looked directly at her.

"Hope. Sit down." He spoke to her, putting all of his focus into the current situation, as she moved to seated. The closest thing to emotion on his face was a slightly raised eyebrow, however otherwise there was not much to indicate what he was about to say. "First of all, no. I do not expect you to go home, which is why I did not take you there." He took a deep breath, before his next point. "Secondly, if I were going to do something awful to you, do you not think I would have already done it? Or at least restrained you so that I could perform said dastardly things later?" He leaned back in his seat. "The moving pictures have corrupted your mind." He rolled his eyes, seeming unamused by her overreaction. "As far as, eating dirt...that is disgusting and untrue." He pulled a book from a nearby position and tossed it onto the table near her.

It made a loud noise in the quiet of the trailer and caused her to jump. She had no idea why he'd tossed it to her, it wasn't like she'd be able to read the script that most of these books were written in anyway. However, she took it and started thumbing through the pages. Most of the notes were in the same language as all of the others, however she did recognise some names of people and places, as well as sketches that had been made amongst the pages.

"So, you're a stalker." She said, closing the book, though this statement came out much calmer than she had been while she was standing.

"No. I am not." His voice was again becoming annoyed, it seemed. He took a hold of the book he'd written in when they arrived, flipping through a few pages until he found the specific page he wanted. He then held it open for her, turning it around so she could see one of the drawings on the page.

She studied the drawing. It was a creature unlike anything she'd ever seen before. It didn't look pleasant, in fact, something about it gave her goosebumps and a chill down her spine.

"So?" She directed the question to him, "What's this? Am I supposed to be afraid of a drawing of some creature you made up and sketched in a book?" Her mind logically told her that nothing like that existed on this Earth and there was nothing to be afraid of, but something else also tugged on her thoughts. Something primitive, left over from before humans went from the hunted to the hunter, something deep inside her begged her to pay attention to the conversation.

"Fantasy is not, nor has it ever been the reason for any of my decisions or creations." He leaned back again with a disinterested gesture of his left hand. "What most do not know about the world, life, and existence in general could fill the vast majority of space twice over. Believe me or not, that does not mean it is not so."

"So why care? Why did you pull me out of its way and not anyone else?" Her wavy purple hair bounced as she gestured frustratedly with her hands, green eyes on fire with emotion. "I don't see a refugee camp in your backyard full of people that you've saved. Or do you have an underground bunker?" She was just being sarcastic now.

"Listen, it is not my choice. It was a favor and I have played my part in it. Do what you like with the information. Take my advice or do not, it really is of no consequence to me." Even though he acted blasé about his answer, she knew there was more to it. He held many secrets, she could see it in his eyes. She still wasn't completely convinced that he was who he said he was, but for now she had nothing to prove otherwise. Until the time that he became dangerous, she figured she'd at least play along. "You are *Talyâ d'Alâhâ.* I have vowed to keep track of and protect said individuals."

She had no idea what the words meant, but it sounded like an old term. With the way he said it, she wasn't sure if she should be concerned or feel better about the situation. She tried to reach deep into her mind to search for having ever heard the words or anything remotely similar. In the end, she simply gave up. Without Google, he was the only person that could tell her what he was talking about and at this very moment, she wasn't sure she even wanted to speak to him anymore. She'd play along for now, until the next time that they might be among civilization, then she'd make a break for it. Until then, she wasn't about to do anything stupid or drastic.

2

Hope awoke to the growling of her stomach and the sun shining through a dirty window directly into her eyes. She squinted and reached her hand up to shield her face from the bright light. She had apparently fallen asleep in the chair that the man had directed she sit in. She remembered watching him write and sketch until the sky outside began to bloom with sunrise. Every word he wrote, though she couldn't understand it, held a fluid beauty, like filigree. She'd never seen writing so beautiful. He could have been writing about the most disgusting thing in the world, but the elegance of the words that were written on each sheet of empty paper filled it with intrigue. However, he was not sitting there anymore. The seat he had been in for most of the night stood empty. His books and papers had been left scattered, without order or organization.

She stood with the intent of finding her host or kidnapper. She was still undecided as to whether she was a guest or a victim at this point. She wandered around the trailer, light now flooding it with a dirt filtered glow. Everywhere she looked she saw more of the same. The trailer was filled with stacks of books with his notes and sketches both loose and tucked inside of said books. Even random things written by others, some old and some new, were scattered about. There wasn't a place within the trailer that she couldn't go, with the exception of a single room. The doorknob seemed to be secured from the inside, but also locked with a padlock from the outside. She wondered how anyone could even enter it, considering it seemed to have no way in. She was curious, but not so much so that she dwelled on the subject for long.

When she couldn't find the man anywhere inside of the trailer, she opened the door and peeked outside toward where he'd parked. The afternoon sun was so bright that she had to squint. The car was still there, in the exact same place, unchanged. She glanced both ways out of the door, as if she were expecting to see him walking along the road. In the light of the day, she could see that it was gravel and long enough to where she couldn't see pavement. There were several reasons that she could think of, as to why he might live so far from a main road. Though most of what her mind could come up with was not anything good.

She pulled herself back into the doorway, closing the door behind her. Glancing around the trailer, she wondered if any of the books here were in English. She figured that most of his notes likely weren't. However, there had to be something that would give her some sort of explanation and whereas she had an undefined amount of time on her hands, she thought a look through everything might help her gain a bit of clarity. Her stomach grumbled once again, but she dismissed it.

She knelt beside a stack of the books, letting her fingers trail along their spines. Most had no titles. Either they had none to begin with or they had worn off. She was looking for something with English on its binding. She kept going, stack after stack, until she finally found something. She could have sworn she'd gone through a hundred of them before she found a single one in a language she could read. There seemed to be many different dialects in the massive amounts of information. This posed the question, how many languages could he read in exactly? She supposed that someone over five-hundred years old could learn quite a bit in that amount of time, but one would think that the human brain would be like a hard drive and run out of storage space eventually.

Her eyes scanned the words on the pages, but even though she could read them, she couldn't actually make sense of them. It wasn't that the information was incomprehensible, it just all seemed like supernatural drivel. Information about angels and demons, halflings both ways, however this information was nothing she'd remembered from Sunday school. There was information about 'Earthbound Hosts', something she had never even heard of before. It spoke of 'Hellfire Hosts', apparently those created in the depths to watch over the gateways to Hell and influence humankind. Hope was confused. As she had previously understood things, that was the position demons were tasked with, much as the next designation in the book she had thought was assigned to angels. 'Heavenly Hosts' was a term she'd heard before, but not in the way this book described it. It spoke of Heavenly Hosts as the inverse of the aforementioned. Hosts created for Heaven that guarded its gates and providing good influence. Just when she had come to the information about the *Talyâ d'Alâhâ,* the term Leo had used, there was a loud noise beside her, causing her to jump.

As she looked up, Hope's eyes fell on a young woman leaning against the doorframe. The girl didn't look in Hope's direction, instead allowed an awkward silence to seep into the air, even though she seemed to be doing it on purpose. The woman was thin, but shapely, her clothing simple and form fitting. Her bright blonde hair was in tight ringlets, held up loosely on top of her head.

"One would think that Leonardo would know better than to leave information out for prying eyes." It was then and only then that the woman's eyes fell on her, and Hope had an awkward feeling, as if she were naked. The woman seemed as if she were peering deep into Hope's soul, somehow without seeing her from the outside, as a normal person would. After doing so, the woman smiled warmly. "Do not be afraid, 'almah , I am not here to chastise you for going through his things. I could truly care less..." She paused, without actually looking at what Hope had been holding, she continued. "...in truth, that information, in particular, could be of great use to you." Without anything else, the woman turned and, within moments, walked back in carrying Leo over her shoulder, like a sack of potatoes. Hope instantly jumped to her feet to try to help the woman, although much to her confusion, the woman didn't seem to actually need help. Hope watched wide eyed and stunned, it took her longer than it should have to wonder exactly why the woman was carrying Leo over her shoulder in the first place. The unknown woman seemed to feel her shock and her eyes moved back to Hope, giving her a half smile.

"I find it amusing..." The woman carried Leo down the hallway, to its dark end, and the locked door. Hope followed out of instinct and a curiosity that seemed ingrained into her. The woman turned her head once she reached the end, glancing toward Hope. "...that you are more surprised and inquisitive about my strength and appearance than you are about the wellbeing of your host."

"That door is locked." Hope pointed out and while she did make a mental note of the woman's astute comment, decided to ignore it for the time being.

"Is it?" The woman gave Hope another half grin, reaching out her finger and pushed the door open without any effort, as if it hadn't even been latched in the first place, the padlock that had locked the outside fell to the floor, broken. The woman carried Leo into the room and almost tossed him on, what appeared to be, the man's bed. However, the same clutter that appeared throughout the house, seemed to be a common theme in here as well. The bed didn't look very slept in, and it was also covered with books and papers, similar to the rest of the house. Like Leo's accent, Hope couldn't place the woman's either, though at least Leo's had been similar to some she'd heard before. This woman's words, though their tone was strong and strict, almost seemed as if she were singing each phrase and they hung in the air as if her voice had its own echo.

Hope glanced around the room; however, she didn't dare touch anything or go any closer to Leo or the woman than a few feet away. The strange, golden-haired woman watched Leo with sadness in her eyes.

"You should not be so hard on him. He is a good man. He has a beautiful soul..." She looked at Hope. "He has been made to stay here for much too long and it has weighed on him." She frowned slightly as she looked back toward him, continuing to watch him. "He has been waiting for you for many years now."

"Me? He's been waiting for me?" Hope blurted out without even thinking before she did so. She was so confused. Why would Leonardo Da Vinci be waiting for her?

"It is just like him that he would not have told you the whole story." She shook her head, then reached out a hand, placing two fingers on his forehead. "Wake up." She spoke forcefully and poked him hard once between the eyes. The touch caused his body to jolt, almost as if she had used a defibrillator.

Leo gasped for air and woke with such force that his eyes sprang wide-open. He coughed, as if it had been the first breath, he'd taken in quite some time. He blinked a few times, then brought his hand to his head.

"Yhidrial. Fancy seeing you here." Leo didn't seem surprised at the woman's presence but *did* seem fairly annoyed. Hope was beginning to believe that it may have simply been the man's personality to appear so.

"You are going to have to do a lot better than that to escape this world, Leonardo." She paused for a single moment, standing. "You know better than to try that nonsense, it did not work in the first five hundred years, and it is not going to work now." She crossed her arms over her chest, watching him. Hope thought she might have stayed around to make sure he would be alright, but something inside her knew that this woman wasn't the type to stay for pleasantries. Even though Yhidrial, as Leo had called her, had said he was good, it didn't seem as though the two were close. Business associates, maybe, but friends would not be how Hope would describe the dynamic between the two now that he was awake. The woman's demeanor had completely changed since the man had gained consciousness.

"I saved her, does He want me to hold her hand for the rest of her life, like the others?" A look of disgust formed over Leo's face, as he sat up in his bed, without looking in either of the women's directions. Neither of them looked in Hope's direction, the two seeming completely wrapped up in their own conversation.

"What is past is making way for that which is to come." The woman stood still, staring at him, unblinking.

"Imagine that. There is always something more. More riddles without answers." Leo took a deep breath, seeming even more irritated at this point.

"If you have a complaint, you will need to take it up with Him. Otherwise, you need not go on your raving lunacy with me, you know I have no control over these things." With this last statement, she turned toward the door of the room and without glancing in Hope's direction promptly went through, disappearing into the clutter of the trailer.

Hope was left speechless, watching Leo, wondering about the conversation, but knowing that this was not the right time to ask him about it. The man didn't look toward her, instead he got up and moved past her, leaving her alone in the room. He went into the 'bathroom' and closed the door behind him. Hope wasn't sure what to make of the situation, so she left the bedroom and made her way toward the main rooms, back to the book she had been looking through before all of the excitement. Yhidrial had said it might be something she should read and within the short time of meeting her, the woman had seemed knowledgeable. Hope wasn't sure she would be able to understand what the book was saying, but at this point, she was willing to try anything to figure out what had happened and what might be going on.

Evening had set in before Leo came back out into the open. Hope watched him for a short while without saying a word, waiting for him to break the silence. She still held onto the book she'd been trying to understand. It was the second time she had gone through the information, trying to make heads or tails of it.

"I know you have been waiting to ask your questions…" Leo spoke without even a single glance toward her. "…so, ask them." He sat down at the table where he seemed to sit quite frequently. He pulled out the book that he'd been writing in previously and began to scrawl some notes in it again. Hope wasn't sure he'd actually answer the questions she had, he sure as Hell hadn't really been very forthcoming in their conversations so far. However, she supposed it didn't hurt to try, especially considering he had told her to ask.

"Who was that woman?" Hope asked him inquisitively.

"Hmm?" Leo seemed puzzled as to why it was the first

question, she asked him and for a moment seemed unsure of what she was talking about, though it wasn't long before he seemed to finally understand. "Ah, Yhidrial." He made a disgusted face before answering. "The bane of my existence, the warden of my preternatural life, the dictator of my immortality." He rolled his eyes, then once again began writing in his book. "She is not really a woman…" He paused for a moment, seeming to be deciding how he wanted to explain things to her. "…at least, she is not human like you are, and I was." He finally turned his gaze toward Hope, narrowing his eyes trying to judge just how much information he needed to give her before her inquiry would be satisfied. "She is Grigori. A watcher." Leo had hoped that this would be enough information for her, but soon he could see that it wasn't. She still had no idea what he was talking about. "By God, have you never set foot in a church, woman?" He seemed to be getting frustrated already. She could tell he wasn't accustomed to explaining himself, but Hope needed him to do so. Even though there were mounds of information at her fingertips, most of it she couldn't read and, what she could read, she couldn't understand. "A Grigori is a designation of angel among the nine choirs. The choirs consist of: Seraphim, Cherubim, Thrones, Dominions, Virtues, Powers, Archangels, Principalities, and then there is the lowest choir that aren't even truly given a title; they are simply angels of no other category. Of course, below them, outside of the choirs, are the Nephilim, then the Heavenly Hosts, and lastly the Earthbound Hosts." He paused, making sure she was taking all of this in. "The latter three we will not discuss at this time, as they are not technically angelic beings, but outside designations. They are more half-breeds, of sorts. On the opposite end of things, there is a similar hierarchy in Hell. We will not go into that now either, we will save that conversation for another time."

Hope listened carefully to what he was saying, were it any other scenario, she might have not listened at all. However, the book that Yhidrial said would be helpful spoke of similar things. She felt as if, were she to truly understand what the book was saying, she would need this background information from Leo. She tried to piece together where she fit into this picture and where Leo fit into it as well, however it was proving to be more difficult than she thought it might be. Hope was an intelligent girl, however most of this was far beyond her level of logical thinking and, at times during their conversations, her brain tried to reject the information. However, here she sat, listening to Leonardo Da Vinci tell her about the classifications of Heaven and Hell. It was all very mind blowing, still she listened intently as he went on.

"The Grigori are a sub-category within the 'generalized' angel group. They are watchers, shepherds of men, and at times do a bit of their own 'miracles', as they see it." Leo frowned as he said this. "Any crazy that says they saw an angel of the Lord have, most likely, seen a Grigori. Very seldom do any of the other choirs visit the Earthly plane, unless it is to rain down fire and sulfur, wiping away 'sin' to start again with a clean slate. Mass destruction and mass miracles are the job of an archangel, there are several, but rarely are they utilized. The other categories have their own small jobs that are routine, but ultimately they all follow His orders." He pointed upward and then paused, trying to figure out where to go next with his explanation. "Grigori do not have enough power to create large scale life or death. A single life 'saved' here and there or an influence to choose the path that He wants a human to choose is basically all they have..." He paused adding a single opinion to his facts. "To be completely honest, I think there is a bit of resentment on the part of some of them, whereas it always seems as if they have a bit of a chip on their shoulder." This would infer that he had met more than just Yhidrial. Hope made a mental note of it, a question she would ask him later, when and if they became close enough to ask more personal questions.

"How do you know these things?" She asked, curious as to whether he'd learned them on his own or if he'd been told by someone who'd seen it.

"That..." He paused, his expression flashing a sadness that she hadn't seen before. "...that is a long story and one for another time." The look that accompanied his answer told her that she had delved into a bit of something personal, so she dropped it for the time being.

"Do they always speak in riddles?" She assumed that asking questions about Yhidrial and angels in general was not off the table, as he didn't seem completely upset with the conversation, just the specific question that she'd asked.

"Both sides are absolutely insufferable at times." Leo rolled his eyes. "They never simply say what they mean..." He paused, using air quotes. "...'influence', not directives." He shook his head. "Though, they are also not the type to mess around with insolence or ignorance. The single positive of the situation is, they seem to have very little concept of the passage of time...which is also a negative, considering one might not hear from them for one hundred years, then one day you will have a divine being on your doorstep, demand-ing to know why the floor is on the floor." He shook his head again. She could tell that he had said it as an extreme example and not an actual situation that had happened, but she under-stood the concept.

"So, Yhidrial...she keeps you alive?" She had known that he had been awakened when she'd touched him but had also gotten from their conversation that he hadn't just been sleeping.

"Alive, yes. Young enough to be useful, no." He moved toward a shelf pulling a small black case off of it. "I made the mistake of thinking that prayer would be all that was needed for them to bring my youth back. After the first hundred years of back pain, arthritis, broken hips, and about every other plight of the aged that you could imagine, I fig-ured it out on my own." He set the case down on the table, opening it, and sliding it toward her, allowing her to see the contents.

Inside were three bottles of the clear liquid, exactly like she had seen him with the other night, a couple of unopened syringes, and a few smaller bottles that had the remains of some sort of pure white powder. The powder was so white that it almost had a glow to it. She looked up toward him after she had analysed the contents. "Are you going to tell me what they are? This is how you reverse the aging process?" She asked him, reaching her hand toward one of the bottles, however he closed it and took it before she could touch it.

"I suppose. You would likely find out anyway, con-sidering this amount will not last long." He put the box back where it had been, seeming as if he might be more particular about where things were, than it might have originally seemed. "The clear liquid is demon venom, mixed with a few herbs to give it direction as to what it is meant to accomplish. The recipe is likely older than the record of time itself, given to the ancient ones to extend life and keep a youthful body to remain productive. The other is angel dust." He let out a small huff of a dry laugh. "Not to be confused with PCP." He grinned to her before continuing. "Angel dust is similar in the way it is used, add a few key ingredients to the ashes of even a single feather and it does the trick. The Bible speaks of the old ones living hundreds of years, this is how they did so." He crossed his arms over his chest. "One is easier to get than the other. Demons are a dime a dozen, there are so many that not all of them are even given names. Angels are fewer than they were before the fall. Aside from the fact, demons build back a new supply of venom within a few days. Angels take, at least, a year to replace a single feather, so as you might guess, they do not give them out frequently. Demon Venom burns quickly. Angel Dust lasts longer." He walked toward a cabinet and pulled out a glass, picking up a skein from the counter near it and poured himself a drink. "Thirsty?" He asked. He hadn't considered that she hadn't had anything to eat or drink since he'd brought her here. He stopped for a moment to ponder the thought but supposed he would deal with the matter later.

Hope nodded, accepting the glass he offered her thankfully. She was hungry but wanted to get all of the information she could from him, before he decided he didn't want to talk any more. Leonardo sat back down with his own glass, ready to continue if she asked him more questions.

"Where would you even get something like that? I mean, it's not like a pharmacy or a grocery store would carry that sort of thing...?" She asked him and even though she understood what he was saying, it still didn't 'make sense'.

"You might not have guessed, but I have my contacts." He took a sip of his glass. "Some of them I am sure you will meet eventually, others likely not. Most are necessary acquaintances, others could possibly be considered friends, of sorts. Of course, until you have chosen a side, the next few weeks should be interesting."

"The next few weeks? Chosen? What are you talking about?" She was taken aback and with every answer that he gave her, she became more confused, and ended up with even more questions.

"Chosen. You know, good versus evil, right versus wrong, angels verses demons, so on and so forth. The age-old choice. Both sides will want you, both sides are going to be nervous of you. At the moment, they both consider you a loaded gun. They will likely play a bit of Russian Roulette with you. First it will start off as a bribe, then fear, then deception, and if all else fails, to them, it is better that neither side has you. Understand?" He tried to look her directly in the eyes to see how much information was actually sinking in.

"What if I never choose a side?" She furrowed her brow, frowning slightly, and meeting his gaze.

He shook his head. "It does not work that way. Everyone chooses a side, it is impossible not to, but free will and all that jazz gives you an opportunity to announce it. You do not even have to say it out loud, generally they can sense it. Yhidrial assumes you are on their side because of your thoughts and concerns for my wellbeing. Also, considering who you are, it is pretty much implied." He shrugged and then took another sip of his glass.

"But who am I though? Why am I so important to any of them?"

"I told you, it is because you are . We will just say you are of 'royal blood'. It is a long story." He leaned back in his seat.

Hope searched through her memories, trying to figure out if she remembered her family saying anything at any point in time that might validate the man's claims.

"Okay then, so what would an angel or a demon want with a human royal? I don't understand why it's so important...what am I next in line to be Queen somewhere or what?" At this point, it all seemed outlandish. Leo and Yhidrial had to have been working together to come up with this story, there had to be something in it for them to make her think she is going crazy or to hold her here, something other than what he was telling her. Something that made more sense.

"You are not seeing the larger picture." Leo sat his glass down and leaned forward. "You are not thinking about the fact that you are dealing with multi-dimensional, semi-immortal beings. You are thinking only in the present, of what you already know, but you need to think about this situation from many different angles. You have to think of the past, the future, up, down, inside, and outside...because that is how they think. They remember everything that has already happened and quite frequently know your decisions before you even make them. They are a part of this world, but also foreign at the same time. It is like an immigrant with a Green Card. They are allowed to be here, but we own this world. They can be deported, but they will eventually return." He stopped, hoping that answer would satisfy her, but even having only known her for a matter of days, he could already tell that it wouldn't.

"You still didn't answer my question. What is a *Talyâ d'Alâhâ* and why is it important? What kind of royal blood? And what does me having royal blood have to do with 'deporting' angels or demons?" A part of her was intrigued, but another part of her said that she should run away from this place and never look back.

"Would you like the scientific explanation or the explanation you will immediately reject as rubbish?" He was watching her closely.

"Both." She said quickly.

"Scientifically, your DNA only has 23 chromosomes, because of what that abnormality means, you have certain traits that are useful to both sides," He paused for a moment before continuing. "Are you sure you want the non-scientific answer?"

"Of course, I'm sure." She crossed her arms over her chest, trying to understand what he'd just said. One would have thought that if the statement were true, a doctor would have found that out by now, so she had already dismissed it as nonsense.

"Alright then, your call," Leo got up, moved several steps toward a pile of books, knocking a few off the top and onto the floor, bringing one back with him to the table. He flopped it down in front of her. She could see that it was a very old, published book, again in another language that she couldn't read. "This book is uncirculated and the only other known copy, the original is in the Vatican archives. It was published in 1467 as the second in a series of two. It only had a single round of publishing. Then on February 3rd, 1468, before another round could be published, Johannes Gutenberg died and almost every copy disappeared."

"How did you get one and what is it?" Hope asked him curiously.

"I know a guy." Leo stated matter-of-factly. "These are the pieces of the New Testament that you are not allowed to see. A good majority does not pertain to our topic, but there are two chapters which are *very* important in explaining this concept to you. Though, considering you are unable to read Hebrew, which it is printed in, you will have to just trust my summary and I will translate you a copy when I am able." Again, he hoped this would be enough for now and, again, he wasn't surprised when it wasn't.

"Okay, so…?" She was getting impatient, suspecting that he was dancing around the question, for some reason. He rolled his eyes, seeming to finally concede.

"The books of Immanuel." He stated through something of a sigh. "First and second Immanuel are detrimental to the Catholic Church, so much so, that they are willing to hide the first-hand words of Jesus Christ to keep the church in power here on Earth." He paused thinking about where he was going to go with this. "Do not underestimate the power of belief. People kill and die to protect what they believe in, there are those that would blindly follow the Catholic Church directly into Hell itself."

"I still don't see what any of this has to do with me." The dots just weren't connecting in her mind...or maybe she didn't want them to. This whole situation was crazy, a part of her expected to wake up from a dream any moment now, but of course she didn't.

"The Bible, as it stands currently, skips quite a chunk of time between Jesus as a boy and Jesus as an adult. In the books of Immanuel, with his own words, he speaks of his family." He watched her to make sure she was following. "His wife and children."

"His wife and kids? The Bible never mentions that he had a family." Now, again, she was even more confused. Leo poked the book in front of her.

"Yes, it did." He leaned back in his chair once more. "The Catholics do not want this information out, because of the power they lose. Imagine the world finding out that there is a direct bloodline to the son of God, the genealogical conformation of God himself, still alive on this Earth. There is absolutely no way that even the Pope could compete with this. The Jews still do not acknowledge that Jesus was, in fact, the Messiah. Then of course, you have the Christians, one never knows which way they will go with this type of information. Christians are like the rebellious stepchild of the church. Most of the time they have no idea what they're doing, but once in a while they get something right." He gave her a 'it is what it is' gesture with his hands. "In other words, to put it in simple terms, many generations back, your grand-father rose from the dead and now that he has gone to build the city of gold, you will be the blood he sheds for this world, princess."

3

——————

Hope's jaw dropped and for a few moments, she was speechless. What can a person really say to that kind of information? Her mind automatically rejected it. When her thoughts were finally collected, moreso than they had been anyway, she jumped out of the seat she'd been sitting in, knocking it over in the process. She backed away quickly, keeping her eyes on him, but swiftly moving toward the door.

"You're crazy...there's no way...it's just not possible..." She stammered almost stumbling as she moved. Da Vinci just sat there, as if he had fully expected this to happen, hung his head, staring at the book in front of him. By the time she got to the door, she almost fell out of it. She didn't say another word. Instead, as soon as her feet hit the ground, she took off in a dead run, as fast as her legs could take her. She had no idea where to go or even where she was at, but there was no way that she was going to stay there one more moment. Who knew what the man's game plan was and how long before he did unspeakable things to her? She was back to the fear of being harmed by him. At this point, it was beginning to border on paranoia, especially considering he'd barely done anything to suggest that he might even be capable of something like that. Still, from everything she'd experienced and how what he'd said was so fantastical. There was no other way she *could* have reacted to it. However, a part of her knew it wasn't a complete fabrication.

After several minutes of sprinting down the unknown road, she began to slow to a jog, then settled into a quick walk. She glanced around. There wasn't anything except trees and the gravel road she was following. Soon she stopped, turning in a circle and looking around. She had absolutely no idea where to go. After looking both ways, forward and back, and seeing nothing, she exasperatedly looked upward. Her shoulders dropped in defeat, and she made her way to the side of the road. She plopped down in the grass. Hope had no idea what to do, her mind sifted through everything within the last couple of days, trying to figure out a game plan. It wasn't long before her concentration was broken by a single male voice. It wasn't Leo. In fact, the voice wasn't familiar at all.

"Bonum mane, Deifilia." It was a pleasant-sounding voice, but something about it gave her a chill down her spine. "Why so flustered?" This man also had an accent she couldn't quite place, but it seemed cockney in nature. It was apparent in the words she had understood. The words she didn't, sounded much more melodic and fluent than those she did. The man walked up beside her and knelt down, so he was on her level. When her gaze met his, she got another chill. The man before her was very handsome, almost too much to be real. There was something odd about him, somehow, she could feel it. His eyes lit up in the darkness, almost as if they had a light behind them.

He was broad, like a high school quarterback, not overly muscular, but seemed as if he was very physically fit. He wore casual clothes, jeans, a t-shirt, and skate shoes. His hair was fairly short but cut neatly and intentionally tousled. She shook her head, her face full of expression, seeming unable to figure out where he'd come from. She hadn't expected anyone to be out here, and it was far too coincidental for him to have just happened along.

"Who are you?" She began to get a bit defensive. She'd already encountered one crazy person; she really didn't want to bother with any more nonsense today. He began to speak again, but when he did, he didn't bother answering her question.

"Ya know ya gotta get used ta thin's, right?" He crouched down beside her, resting his arms on his knees. "Ya lucky I found ya before a Pale Rida's and Featha's." He tilted his head, seeming to study her and commit her features to memory.

"Who are you?" She repeated, squinting while looking at him, not only because she was suspicious, but from where she was sitting, the sun was in her eyes. To which she was answered by a charming grin and the tap of a finger on the tip of her nose, almost as if he found her cute. Not cute like a guy would find a girl, but almost like a human would find a puppy. It was very obvious to her now that this man *wasn't* simply someone who had happened along.

"Ya quite somethin', ya know.?" He put one hand

to the ground, lowering himself to take a seat next to her. He picked up a rock, holding it in a clenched fist while he continued speaking to her. "I'm not important, not in a grand scheme a thin's anyhow." He shrugged, looking out over the road. "One a the lower levels. We keep an eye on The Architect too, ya know." He nudged her lightly and playfully with his elbow. He didn't exactly say which side he was on, just that he was a lower level. "Outta the featha's and into a fire. Right, love?" He chuckled lightly, then shrugged. "Ya all get used to it, there's been Blood before ya...an' there'll be Blood after ya gone." He paused for a split second, before shrugging and addressing her again. "Ya will too, Deifilia."

"You're from..." She didn't want to say something that might offend him, what he'd told her only leading to more questions. She hadn't been able to ask any questions of Yhidrial, now having every intention of trying to get information from this man...or whatever he was, before he disappeared. "You're a demon? Or a devil? Or..." She put her hand on her forehead, confused about the whole situation and very overwhelmed at this point. She was met with another breathy laugh from him, to which she dropped her hand to her lap and glared at him.

"Ah nah, doll." His smile was intoxicating, and Hope could see how humans could get in over their heads with someone like him. "I 'aven't a luxury a titles, think a me like a erran' boy for a mob...but like nothing ya ever seen before, right?" He brought his hands up, gently rolling the rock between his palms.

"Okay, so what do you keep calling me? Day-fee-a? That is not my name." The thought crossed her mind that maybe they had gotten the wrong girl. It would make sense to her, and she would welcome the opportunity to have her mind erased and the ability to go back to her normal life.

"Deifilia? Means, Daughter a God." He stopped rolling the rock around in his hands. "In Hellspeak. Enochian's simila'. Once ya know one, ya basically know 'em both. Kina like Latin, s'pose is a reason why it's mostly a dead tongue. Is much too close for comfort of a church. Can't be speakin' ta firemouths. Can't learn a language a angels, humans ain't worthy. 'Sides, humans knowin' 'bout a truth, means a church can't control ya like they do. Bird brains dunna come down a see a underlin's. They much prefer they're high horses an' ignorin' dad's bastard kids." He gave her a wink as if he'd just shared a secret and motioned toward her, suggesting that humans were the 'bastard children' that he was talking about.

Just when she was about to ask him another question, she heard a familiar voice coming from a short distance of the direction she had come from.

"Sam." It was something of a greeting, recognition going beyond formal. It wasn't quite friendly, but it didn't seem as if they were enemies either.

"Leo, o' boy, how's life an' it?" The man slowly stood from the ground, brushing himself off. "We've a new *Talyâ d'Alâhâ*. She be the last one, ya think? Think we needin' a be ready for a fall an' brawl?" He brought his fists up, throwing a couple of punches at the air, as if he were mocking some sort of fight. The look on Leo's face didn't seem to be amused. "Oh, come off it, o'boy. Lighten up, maybe this 'en she'll soften ya spirit. She does 'ave quite a light. Be interestin' a see what she does wit' it." He spoke about her as if she wasn't still sitting beside them on the ground.

Hope crossed her arms over her chest in a frustrated pout, glancing from one man to the other. Sam glanced toward her with a half grin.

"Be careful a this 'en, Deifilia…he's a wily sort, ya know what I mean…" Sam let out a short laugh once more, then tossed the rock that he'd been holding toward her. She caught it; however, it wasn't a rock any longer. It was something more. What she now held in her hand was a perfect marble-esque sculpture. It was a smoothly shaped ring and though it looked like it might fit her, she didn't dare put it on. She looked up toward him with confusion as to how he had done the trick and why he had given it to her. His eyes replied with a sense of recognition. He either had known that she would have questions or had experienced this scenario before.

"We are what we are, but who we are isn't defined by what we are." Sam repeated a quote, seeming to force more proper English for the phrase, but she didn't think she'd ever heard the phrase before. "Ya get inna trouble, ya just give a call, right? Just 'cause ya 'aven't made a side don't mean we gotta be automatic foes." He glanced toward Leo. "If ya work for a otha side, don't mean we gotta be neither. Many areas a light an' dark in this war, but ya find there's many more a in-between." He looked back toward her again, then gave her one more playful wink. "Leo, he'll show ya how a use it." With that last phrase and a flash of light, his physical form disappeared, as if thin air had opened him up and swallowed him. Hope, still holding the marble ring in her hand, sat there shocked staring at the place where the man had been, having never seen anything like it before.

"Sam, as I am sure you have deduced, is not quite your average individual." Leo said, turning and beginning to walk back toward the trailer. He knew she would follow, if she didn't, she would never have her questions answered.

Leo was, in fact, absolutely correct in his assumption. However, much to his frustration, her questions did not wait until they were back in the trailer.

"Sam? He said he's an errand boy for the mob...what does that mean? He said, even if I pick the other side, we don't have to be enemies...? From what you told me; it certainly seems we should be. How do I know the difference and that I've picked the right side?" Hope didn't seem to be finished by the time Leo turned around, his eyes beaming with annoyance.

"Yes, Sam. Abbreviated for modern times, much like mine. His given name is Samael." He paused, seeming to choose his words carefully. "Sam is complicated." Her last questions finally hit his last nerve, for whatever reason, his response to it was much different than the previous. "You will know the way you have always known. Do you truly believe you have gotten this far on your own, for better or for worse?" For a moment, he seemed to forget to answer one of her questions. "As for enemies and who is within each category, I suppose we will have to discuss that sooner rather than later." By the time he'd finished, he was at his doorstep and went back into the trailer without another word. When Hope walked through, she immediately noticed him rummaging through his books and papers. After several minutes of looking, he seemed to find what he was looking for and move toward the table to sit.

Hope had already taken a seat, assuming he would probably go back to writing, as he did before at this table. He did not. Instead, he thumbed through the pages for a few moments, then turned the book around and slid it to her. There were detailed images, some almost lifelike portraits, some symbols. The words were in another language and the portraits were unlike any creatures she'd ever seen before.

"This. This is what you are up against, this is the choice you'll have to make." He paused when Hope's eyes went wide, staring at the page. "You will likely never see a single one of these as they are on this page. They will look normal to you. Plain everyday individuals." He took a brief moment to point to one image in particular. Hope stared at it for a few moments taking in what he was trying to say. "This is a depiction of Sam."

Hope looked from the book to Leo, then back. "I don't understand."

Leo removed his hand from the book, leaning back in his chair, folding his hands together. Hope kept staring at the page, trying to understand the conversation she'd had earlier and put this new information together with it. She was still quite confused; it became very clear to her that she needed Leo. This was his world and now she was in it whether she liked it or not. It had become apparent that she couldn't get away from it, by getting away from him. She would certainly rather have him with her, if nothing else, for a frame of reference, than try to take on this entire new existence on her own. Even if she wasn't sure whether her role in this situation was exactly what had been told to her, she was certain that she wouldn't last long on her own.

"As I said..." Leo glanced back down at the book for a moment, then back up at her. "...complicated. To be completely honest, you will find 'complicated' a lot more frequently than you ever will clear cut. Sam is a lot of things, but you will not find many who know more of life, this world, and the next, than he...on both sides of the proverbial coin."

Hope placed her fingertips on the page, tracing very old lines of ink. "Both sides?" The image was a contradiction to the conversation with Sam. The conversation with Leo raised even more questions. "This is what he really looks like...? Should I trust him? Is he good or evil? What side is he on?"

"Yes. Both sides." Leo closed his eyes in annoyance at her current onslaught of questions, putting his fingertips to his temples. He couldn't understand why she always insisted upon asking so many questions at once. Polite company would allow one the opportunity to answer, before continuing a line of questioning. This age truly was lacking, in his opinion. "Sam is in a fairly broad category. It encompasses many types of beings and things. However, that is a bit of a tangent, unnecessary to go into at this time. So, the answer to your next question is obvious. No, not all within this category look such as these. Some do, some do not. In fact, very few do, in this particular case." He paused for a moment, letting this part sink in, before he went into the specifics of Sam. "As far as Sam is concerned, the answer is yes and no. It truly depends on what you intend on trusting him with." When it was clear she did not intend on looking at it any longer, he took the book and closed it, sliding it away on the table. "Good or evil? That truly depends on who you ask and what standards you are holding him to."

"Okay so, shade of grey. Understood." Hope was still very confused. "Why was he speaking Hellspeak when he clearly started out playing for the other team?" She was referring to the image in the book. Among all of the hideous monster creatures, a few images depicted angelic beings, Sam was one of those creatures.

"He did. Sam is one of the Fallen." Leo placed a hand on the thick book. "This image depicts before the Fall. Many fell. Many perished. Many faded into the background and are no longer players in this cosmic game. Before the thriving of humanity, a holy civil war began. A rebellion. A mutiny. Sides were chosen. Angel against angel, for the rule of Heaven." Leo shook his head. "To be fair, it was a very ignorant war. I do not believe that Lucifer thought his position out well. While they do not grow old, nor sick, nor frail...they can still be killed. To rise up against a true immortal, the creator of everything in existence, they were destined to fail. Lucifer, much like Hitler, is a salesman. We will discuss Lucifer at another time though. Samael, needless to say, made the wrong choice. As a punishment, those who had sided with Lucifer and those who chose not to fight were cast from Heaven and here they must remain until Judgement. After which, it is said they will spend their eternity in Hell."

Parts of the story still didn't make sense to Hope. "So, he's evil?" She asked.

"I did not say that." Leo replied. "Gray area, remember? You see, Sam...before the war, was charged with very specific jobs. He was 'Dei Malleo' or 'Elenin ', The Hammer of God. In simple terms, he was God's enforcer. By the time war broke out in Heaven, Sam could not take it any longer. I believe you call it PTSD. He had seen and caused the suffering of so many living beings on Earth, he could not bear to watch his brothers and sisters die also. He made the decision not to fight, but for that he was punished. Now, he has been banished from Heaven, as one of the Fallen. However, in truth, he assists both sides. Though, generally speaking, he tends to lean much more Team God, than Team Lucifer. Sam accepts his fate, he has had to, but his heart craves righteousness and the triumph over evil. It was how he was created to be, and unlike others, he does not fight what is in his nature to be."

Hope nodded. It made a bit more sense now, she supposed. At least where Samael was concerned. Suddenly a slow clap began from the corner of the room.

"Leo, ya drama's quite astoundin', ya know. Really. Two thum's way, way up." Sam sarcastically gave Leo a thumbs up. "There's a bit more to it, a plot line's there, but we lef' out a bit a details, 'aven't we?" Sam winked at Leo, who rolled his eyes. "I don't 'ave a Post Trauma Disorder neither. I'm a lova not a fighta." Sam grinned, bringing his hand to his heart.

"I thought you left." Leo let out a deep breath, rolled his eyes and crossed his arms over his chest. "If I would have known to expect company, I would have put the kettle on and let you explain the whole mess yourself." This was obviously sarcastic, whereas Leo didn't even own a tea kettle, that Hope had seen.

"Jiminy Christmas, mate...ya still butt hurt 'bout that nigh' in San Lucas? Paco said she was legit..." Sam raised an eyebrow, giving him a jokingly charming grin, before his eyes shifted to Hope for just a moment. "...I bailed ya out, didn't I?"

Leo didn't seem amused. "After three days, dying of dehydration. They say not to drink the water and I did not feel like taking a chance, in a cage, with seven other 'hombres'." Leo rolled his eyes and shook his head. Sam's expression went solemn, before he said something to Leo that Hope didn't understand.

"Deus his opus habet videre in mane coram. Vocationem Yhidrial hoc est, non velle puer per Deum ." Almost immediately, Sam had Leo's attention, true annoyance crossing over his face.

"I will not call her into this." Leo replied. The only word that Hope recognized was Yhidrial's name in the jumble of what might as well have been complete nonsense, from what she could understand. By Leo's response, Hope was unsure who he was talking about. She gave Sam one point, for communicating without trying to. Leonardo zero, for being as absolutely vague as possible.

"Grab your things, we are going to town." Leo spoke to Hope without so much as looking at her, seeming more frustrated than normal. "I assume you're coming, as well?" He was met with a simple shrug from Sam.

"I've got nowhere more pressin' a be." He was trying to give off the appearance that he didn't care one way or another, but supernatural being or not, Hope picked up on subtle cues. She couldn't be sure as to why he wanted to be around them and with him resting firmly between good and evil. She would have to remember to stay on her guard. "Shall we then?" Sam tried to use his appeal to mask whatever he was thinking and feeling, offering her his arm as if to escort her. Leo on the other hand had already made his way out of the door and was proceeding to start the car. Hope hesitantly took Sam's arm, feeling very awkward about it, but oddly it made her feel almost like a princess to be walked to the car. Sam opened and closed the car door for her, before hopping into the back seat.

"What do you think you are doing?" Leo addressed Sam for the first time since he'd decided they were leaving. Before, he had been so in his head that it barely seemed to register that Hope was sitting beside him. It was obvious that Leo had assumed Sam would be taking his own mode of transportation.

"I'm along for a ride, bud." Sam made himself at home in the back seat, cranking down one of the windows as he did so. He laid back, crossed his feet at the ankles, putting them up on the center console, then lit up what looked like a rolled cigarette. Leo didn't seem to be thrilled with multiple parts of this scenario, but he didn't seem as if he had the concentration or the willpower to argue about it.

The car ride wasn't long, as far as car rides go. Though the silence was almost entransic amongst the hum of the old motor. Sam lightly tapped a rhythm in the back seat, while whistling a hushed melody that Hope had never heard before. She could also tell with each moment that went by, every small thing that Sam did was slowly escalating Leonardo's annoyance. She just hoped they made it where they were going, before Leo decided to pull the car over and murder their resident Fallen.

It wasn't long before they pulled up to, what seemed to

be an empty lot, however Hope wouldn't have known it if she hadn't been awakened by the screeching of the old car's brakes. Somehow, she had fallen asleep, though she hadn't remembered feeling tired when they had gotten into the car. She didn't question it much, considering car rides in the dark were known to cause passengers to fall asleep and it had been a stressful few days. Though, something between Leo and Sam had changed since she had been asleep. She assumed that Leo had finally gotten enough of Sam's antics and had said something, because even though Leo still seemed annoyed, Sam was a bit more rigid and less aloof.

"He's not gunna like 'er in there. Better go in an' we'll wait out 'ere." Sam spoke to Leo, as if he hadn't truly wanted to, but seemed genuinely concerned for Hope's wellbeing. Leo huffed, seeming unconvinced. "Ya know a feathers can't protect 'er in there an' till she's decided, they ain't gunna do much anyhow." Leo knew he was right.

"Fine." Leo finally agreed. "Stay here." Leo spoke knowing full well that Hope wouldn't listen to him, so he tossed a glare toward Sam that seemed to mean something, then quickly got out of the car.

Almost as soon as Leo stepped from the car, Sam moved around in the back seat, causing Hope to turn her head and instinctively look toward him. However, she quickly looked back in the direction Leo had gone, but he had disappeared.

" 'bout time, thought boy-o would neva get gone." Sam leaned forward, his handsome and perfect grin beaming from the back seat. "Ain't one for followin' orda's, eh love." Before Hope could protest, Sam laid a hand on her shoulder, and everything went black for a few moments.

When Hope's vision began to slowly clear, all she could see was a bright light and then things began to come into focus. Sam was holding onto her, so she didn't fall and her whole body felt numb and tingled. She pushed away from Sam, stumbling backward, angry with him for doing whatever he had done to her.

"Calm it, Deifilia." Sam motioned to her by putting his hands up in surrender. "Is always disorientin' a firs' time." Hope tried to catch her bearings, looking all around her and gathering information about where they were. She was breathing heavy, like her lungs couldn't hold much air. However, she could tell that everything was beginning to go back to normal...even though she was beginning to feel like she was going to throw up.

"What did you...do to me?" She spoke to him through deep breaths, when she could finally form words. She squinted her eyes, still looking around at everything. "A tattoo shop? What are we getting bestie tattoos now or something?" Her words were sarcastic and after them, she heard a deep laughter coming from another room. Her eyes quickly moved from Sam to a doorway nearby.

"You could say dat, cher." The man who appeared from the other room had such dark skin that in the dim lighting, one could only see the whites of his eyes and the brightness of his glistening, toothy grin. As the man came closer, Hope found herself lifting a hand to him, without even thinking about it. An action, to which the man slipped his own hand under hers, bowing in greeting and placing a kiss to it, in formal greeting, as if he had expected her to offer it to him. "Laurent Saint Arnaud...pleasure." As he let her hand go, Hope finally realized that it wasn't just an impression that she'd gotten. He had known she'd do it, because he had caused her to. Hope backed a step away, glancing toward Sam, like a deer being fed to a wolf.

"Not a worry, girlie. Laurie here, plays both sides too. Highest bidder, right?" Sam gazed toward the man. "That'd be us." Sam placed a hand on her shoulder and squeezed lightly.

"I ain't a got all day, Sam. Next appointment's in t'irty minutes. Time is money, bro'dah." Laurent had a very thick accent, one that seemed old and with Haitian creole origins. Laurent motioned toward a clock, one that Hope hadn't really noticed was there until he had motioned to it, which made her wonder if it had even been there at all or if he had made it appear just then.

"You an' I both know it won't take no thir'y minutes a get this one thin' done." Sam shook his head, reaching around Hope and keeping his arm there, as he led her toward where Laurent was standing. To which Laurent once again grinned, shrugging lightly.

"You right, but de Missus she 'bout done wit mah dinneh and I dun a wan' it ta get col'." He tossed Hope a wink, before raising both of his hands, whispering something that Hope didn't quite catch, and then more quickly than she even had time to think pushed her backward with both hands on either side of her collarbones . Sam, who seemed to be expecting the shove, held her from falling backward and then reached around to catch her in case she fell forward. Beneath where Laurent's palms had been, felt as if she'd just gotten the worst sunburn of her life. However, without allowing her time to think about it, Sam gave a quick thank you salute to Laurent and once again Hope blacked out.

When Hope began to come to again, even before her vision cleared, she balled her fists, ready to lay into Sam. She saved it, considering when she was able to see straight, she realized they were not alone in the car anymore. Leo must not have realized that they had been gone, because she was sure he would have been furious if he'd known what had happened. She'd gotten the distinct impression that Leo was not the type of person that liked being out of the proverbial loop. For now, she'd wait and cry on the inside about how much her shoulders were hurting. She looked into the back seat and gave Sam a glare, letting him know that she wasn't going to forget it any time soon. To which, he gave her an 'oops' gesture and shrug. He did not seem to care that she was angry with him, which also seemed odd, because since she'd met him, he had shown more concern for her than anyone she had met within the last few days.

It wasn't long before they were, all three, back at the trailer where they had started out. Leonardo turned the vehicle off, without a word, seeming still distracted, and made his way back to the house. Hope stared at the door when he closed it, knowing Sam was still in the back seat, his eyes on her. Hope watched the darkness outside, using the silence to emphasise how upset she was with him. Though, to be fair, she wasn't as mad now as she had been. Her shoulders still stung from whatever the tattoo man had done, it was more than simply a surface pain, she felt it through her body. She knew he hadn't done anything simple, likely it had something to do with this whole mess, she just needed to figure out what.

"I don't know what you did, but I didn't like it." She finally said to him.

"Was a last-minute decision." It wasn't really an excuse; he didn't seem to be looking to pass blame. "Ya don't understand this world, love. It'll eat ya alive if ya not ready…" He paused for a split second. "…an' ya not ready." There was almost a sadness to his tone.

"So what? Whatever that guy did is supposed to make me ready?" She asked him, her attitude seeming again frustrated.

"No.' His voice was very matter-of-fact. "But it never hurts a see what's comin' after ya." As he said this, he slid out of the car and opened her door. "Let's take a walk."

She was unsure about the situation, but as much as she didn't trust him, especially now, she also felt as if there was something to him, just beneath the surface. She took the hand he had outstretched to her, allowing him to help her out.

"Fine…" She didn't stand there for long before she began walking, without paying attention to what he was doing, but she was sure he remained a couple of steps behind her. Hope stopped where the two had first met, at the side of the road and just as she had done before, she plopped herself down in the grass. She watched him as he slowly and carefully sat down beside her and for a while they just sat there, the music of nature slowly beginning to lull Hope into calmness.

"I did it a protect ya." He stared into the darkness of the woods. "Laurent, he's good at what he does, most don't even know he has a hand a play. 'Ell, I don't even know all that 'e knows." He motioned to the trailer. "Ya see, we been watchin' from a sidelines, waitin' on a new'en to be called. A Talyâ d'Alâhâ, as the featha' call 'em. Puer Deus, down unda..." he stopped. "...an' not Australia, neither." He glanced toward Hope, who was still staring forward expressionless. "I know it's hard a understand. Ta us, it's kinda like an experiment. This is a first time we caught one of a the Blood ahead a decision," He stopped, remembering something. "Didn't ya said ya met Yhiddy?" Sam seemed confused. "Wonda why she didn't throw 'er 'at in a ring."

"So, you marked me? Does that mean I don't get a choice anymore?" Her voice was trembling with her frustration escalating again.

"Ain't nothin' like that," He stood, " Offering her his hand to help her up. "Besides...it ain't even active yet." Quicker than she could stop him, with somewhat unnatural speed, Sam somewhat repeated what Laurent had done. However, when his palms landed on the fresh burn marks it was much different.

His hands stuck there, like a magnet, and beneath them lit up like Vegas. She could feel the white light pulsating through to the other side of her like a bolt of lightning. However, there was no pain or burning, only the feeling of pure energy, exploding into her body like a dam breaking.

4

Hope had been so taken aback that she hadn't even realized she had been standing there, with her eyes closed and her mouth wide open. When her mind had once again come back, she was furious.

"What the Hell was that? What did you do? You seriously need to stop..." She had been so angry that she hadn't even noticed that her world had completely changed in those few moments. Shocked, she looked Sam up and down. His countenance was very similar, but as if a light were shining behind him, his whole body was fully immersed in bright, white light.

Sam rolled his shoulders like he carried the weight of the world on them and when he did so, the shoulder joints of a set of wings could be seen. She couldn't see actual wings behind him, but she assumed they were there. He watched her with a sadness, the kind that only surfaced in cases of repressed pain.

"Ya won't see 'em." He seemed to be speaking to her reaction. "They ain't there." He lifted the appendages to show her. Where his wings used to be, was left only two amputated knobs, wrapped from shoulder blades to broken tip with grey, medical grade wrappings. He had been telling the truth, what she could now see made her feel terrible for him and so she sat back down in the grass. She curled her legs up so she could hug them and rest her forehead on her knees. Sam sat down beside her, unsure of what to do at this point.

"Sorry, Deifilia." He wrapped his arm around her and tried to pull her closer to lean on him. He had considered the possibility of her throwing a punch instead, but it had been worth the risk. Instead, she leaned exactly as directed, beginning to lightly sob. "I know is a lot a take in, but you'll get it. Not a end of a world...yet." His hand softly trailed her back, "Can't do much, but what I know might get ya through. Not a lon' term fix but might help wit somethin'."

Eventually her crying died down and for a moment, she wondered why Leo hadn't come looking for her. Whatever meeting he'd had while they were with Laurent, must have been extremely important. She lifted her head off of Sam's shoulder, looking up to him. He seemed as if he had been watching her the whole time and he was still running his hand down her back to soothe her.

Within a short time after Sam began consoling her, she straightened up, pulling away from him. She still wasn't exactly sure of where he sat on the scale of good versus evil and, for that matter, exactly where she sat either.

"So, what did Laurent do to me?" She thought it was a fairly straight forward question and that she deserved to know what it was that had been forced upon her by the two of them. Sam considered her question for a bit, before he answered her.

"So, look at 'umans like a locked door, yeah? Ya know what ya see on a side, an ya know there's probably somethin' on a otha side. Ya can look in a keyhole. Ya can look in a peephole. But ya neva really see a 'ole picture or know what's on a other side until ya unlock a door an' open it." He stopped for a second gesturing to her still sore shoulders. "Magic Man an' I, we gave ya a skele'n key."

"What's that supposed to mean? So, I have like super-powers or something now?" She was still confused, a part of her knew what he was saying, but another part completely rejected any of the last couple of days as reality. Sam shook his head.

"No supa powers, love. Jus' given ya a sight, s'all. Let's ya see through a bullshit storm that both sides pull ova ya. You get mosta what I got, which ain't really nothing but a sight itself." He looked away from her and up to the sky. "Not sup-posed a do it, ya know. Ya supposed a make a way on ya own, make a decision on ya own, but putin' it plainly, Deifilia...lots a us, we're ready for a end to it all." He kept watching the sky like he was expecting something to happen.

"The end? You mean like the end of everything or just the fighting?" She was becoming very curious about him, and she truly didn't know much, only what Leo had said and what Sam himself had spoken of.

"Does it matta'? A end of a fightin' means a side is won, which ain't nothin' good." He looked back to her. "Ever thin' exists in a delicate balance, throw that off an' everythin' falls apart. Can't be one without a otha. Won't matta for me, I know where I'm headed...but ya still gots a choice an' a chance. Make it a good'en, 'cause He don't like indecision an' bowin' out of a fight ain't a option." He spoke as if he'd had some experience with such things. She could feel and see such a deep sadness in him. Hope didn't know him well enough to pry or console him, so she just left it alone. "Some a us are jus' tired, ready a stop waitin' for the gran' finale. I got my sentence, now I'm ready a serve it." He took a deep breath that ended in a sigh, then began to stand. "I gotta get goin', few pressin' issues a take care of," he held a hand out to help her up. She took his hand to get up, but let go as soon as she was on her feet. He didn't seem surprised, but she thought she saw a small twinge of disappointment in him. "Put a ring I gave ya on. If ya need me, I'll be 'ere. No tricks. Promise." He raised his hands up, to gesture his innocence in the matter. "I jus' wanna 'elp. If ya worried, ask Leo 'bout it. Maybe a lotta things, but I ain't no liar." He began to walk toward the trailer, intending to escort her to the door like a gentleman. She pulled the ring out of her pocket, however when she did so, she realized it was different with her newly gained sight.

There were symbols on it, glowing with a very similar light to the one in which Sam himself had given off. They glowed from the inside, almost like a lighthouse in the dark. The inscription was definitely not in English. Yesterday, it would have looked like squiggles to her, but today some- how, she could read it. The words were, 'סמאל, פטיש האל', loosely translated it read, 'Samael, the Hammer of God.'

Sam stood beside the stairs, as she made her way up them, watching her like he wanted to say something. Instead, he seemed to change his mind and reroute his thinking to some- thing safer.

"Don' a be afraid of a key, Deifilia. They be a lot a thin's ya be noticin' ya can see an do now, too much a be makin' a list. Jus' roll wit' it, eh?" To an extent, he truly seemed nervous about his decision to give the power to her. She nodded reaching toward the door. "He don't know I did it a ya, so wait as long as ya can a tell 'im. What he knows, they know." He pointed skyward. "They got 'im on a tighta leash than they got you..." he paused to frown, "...an' trust me, they got ya tighter than ya know. They don't like losin' they kin t' a dark side." She once again nodded with understanding, then went inside.

She expected Leo to be sitting where he had been the last couple of days, but he wasn't. Instead, he'd left the lamp on for her, and he was nowhere to be found. She glanced down the hallway and unsurprisingly there was a crack of light beneath the door that was his bedroom. Rolling her eyes, she glanced around trying to find somewhere to lay down or some sort of food. She hadn't eaten since Leo had brought her here. She also felt disgusting, considering she hadn't showered or changed clothes either.

After finding nothing to eat, nowhere to sleep, and getting overall frustrated, she decided to try to get Leo's attention. She should have asked Sam to take her to her home, but she hadn't thought about it before he left. She might have called him back, rather than asking Leo, had Sam not said he had something to do. Whatever it was, she wasn't even sure if she wanted to know. After watching the door to Leo's bedroom for a few moments, she finally decided the man was already grouchy enough on a normal basis, let alone being disturbed in the middle of something. She glanced around the trailer, looking for any signs of the keys to the car. She certainly didn't intend on walking however far the road was, and she didn't currently have a working phone to call an Uber. She moved a few things around on the table, thinking that maybe the keys might be under some papers or a book. No luck. She wandered around aimlessly, looking anywhere logical that she could think of. It was only when she finally gave up that she caught a brief glint of metal, on the floor, under the table.

She shook her head, rolling her eyes. She should have known they wouldn't be in any place logical or intentional. During the very short amount of time that she had known the guy, Leo hadn't once seemed to really plan much out. He obsessed over things. He fell easily into his own world. He was easily distracted. These were just a few observations she'd made in two days' time. Though, something told her that there was more to the man than what one saw on the surface.

She picked the keys up off of the floor and made her way to the vehicle, hopping in and starting it up. She didn't think Leo would probably notice the sound of the car starting, but she wasn't going to give him the chance to protest. She was going home. At this point, she didn't intend on staying there for long. She intended to grab a few things and then come back to the trailer. She was stubborn, but she wasn't stupid. In a world with confirmed angels, demons, and monsters, she didn't think she stood a chance on her own. She needed the two men she had met, the jury was still out on the woman angel, Yhidrial.

It didn't take long to get to her apartment. In fact, she hadn't realized just how close the trailer was to where she lived. It had only taken ten minutes to get to a main road and from there, she knew exactly where she was. After a fifteen drive, beyond the gravel, she pulled up to her building, parking out front and making her way upstairs. She didn't have her keys, in fact, she wasn't even sure where they were at this point. They had not been the most important things on her 'keep track of' list. However, she had learned to always keep a hide-a-key, as she had locked herself out far too many times to count. When she reached her door, she lightly kicked the crown molding, causing a small section of it to fall and reveal a key taped beneath it. She plucked it off of the wall and let herself into her home.

Once she was inside, she took a deep breath. It was just how she'd left it. The way it smelled, the familiar sounds that the old building made, it almost made her feel normal. She put the keys to Leo's car down on her kitchen counter, making a mental list of things she needed to do before she left and items she needed to grab. First and foremost, though, she needed a shower. Before any more craziness, she needed to relax, to process everything that had happened, and just breathe.

Hope pulled several things from her drawers, mostly comfortable clothes. There was no point to dressing up, simply to go back to a dusty, dirty trailer. As she was doing so, she heard the familiar soft footsteps of her long-time companion. She bent down, placing a loving hand on her cat having missed him a great deal within the last couple of days. The cat, in turn, shrugged her off, seeming frustrated with her for having been gone and walked a few steps away from her.

"Oh, come on, Set. You're not really mad at me," She dropped down to the floor, reaching her arms out to the feline. "You were fine." The cat seemed to snub her, continuing to walk away into the other room, as if he just wanted to let her know how angry he was. She rolled her eyes. Her crazy cat was always so temperamental and dramatic.

After she was satisfied with the clothing she had chosen to wear after her shower, she made her way to her bathroom and dropped her dirty clothes on the floor. Suddenly she was caught off guard. It was the first time she'd seen herself undressed since the tattoo shop. However, now she could see it hadn't been a tattoo he'd given her. She moved closer to the mirror, inspecting the symbols that were there. Both sides were similar, but not quite the same. On her left, was a Pentagram. On her right, was a Triquetra. Symbols of both sides, good and evil. They were unlike anything she'd ever seen before. They were not tattoos. They were not a brand. Hope brought her hand up and traced the line of the triquetra with her fingertip. They were still a little sore, but not unbearably so. The skin was not broken. If a wound had ever been there, there was no sign of it now. She turned and glanced over her shoulder at her back. By their appearance, it was almost as if a proverbial cookie cutter had cut the symbols all the way through her body and within the empty spaces a light similar to Sam's burned bright. When the symbols were not lit, they merely looked like deep, dark holes cut into her body. You couldn't see through them. You couldn't see her internal systems, muscles, or bones. They were solid black and empty.

After she'd had her fill of inspecting them, she settled her mind knowing that at least she would never have to be afraid of pure darkness again, not as long as her body made its own light. She was still a bit frustrated with Sam for having forced them on her, but from what he'd told her, it was for good reasons. However, she did wonder how much one could actually trust one of the Fallen. Leo seemed to think that it depended on the situation. Though, Hope was still unsure how she would know the difference.

The shower water felt amazing against her skin, the almost scalding water pouring over her whole body. She'd always been a fan of showering in water as hot as her body could tolerate and it was routine for her to step out of it with skin so red that it could have been mistaken for sunburn. This was one of those times. She watched as the steam from the shower drifted up into the air around her. It was always so serene to stand there in the shower, the sound of the water flowing and pitter-pattering against the tub. It never truly lasted long enough, whether she was in there for five minutes or an hour.

Upon finishing, she stepped out into an almost eerie quiet. The apartment wasn't making noise. There were no sounds coming from outside. Set was not even crying or complaining about being hungry, as he frequently did. She quickly wrapped a towel around her and walked out into the main area of the apartment. Hope narrowed her eyes, scanning for anything out of place. She couldn't see anything wrong. Dismissing it, she walked back to the bedroom to get dressed. She didn't make it all of the way there before something grabbed her from behind. She squealed quietly and reached up to where she thought she felt hands, but there were no hands holding her, she only ended up touching her own skin. She held onto her towel for dear life, so it stayed in place as much as possible during the ordeal. It was then that she realized she was not wearing the ring Sam had given her. She'd left it in the bathroom with her other jewelry. Whatever had her in a tight grip her tight and wasn't letting go. It began to pull her toward the living room window, which she suddenly realized was open. Oddly enough, her first thought was not about her safety or trying to figure out what was going on. Her first thought was that she hoped this entity had not let her cat out.

Though it was mere seconds in real time, being dragged helplessly toward the window, by an invisible force, seemed like an eternity. It pulled her close enough that she could almost touch the window frame and feel the chill of the breeze that flowed in from the outside. She looked over the ledge at the pavement three stories below. If she was pushed out, the likelihood of surviving the fall was slim. She began trying to struggle, trying to get away, but the more she fought, the tighter it grasped her. Her body began to tense up and closed her eyes. In anticipation of the fall, as she could feel herself being shoved forward.

Without an ounce of remorse or hesitation, Leo burst into the apartment at the perfect moment.

"Mahkh-SOHM!" Leo yelled holding his hand out in the direction of the window. If Hope hadn't had the symbols, she would have never understood what Leo had said. But as it stood, she knew that he'd sent a shield to keep the concealed thing from pushing her out. With the barrier now in place, Leo rushed forward, lifting some sort of cylinder to his lips and blowing through it. In turn it made a popping noise, a white powder blowing from it, and filling the small area around them all with a thick cloud.

The dust settled quickly, but instead of falling through the creature, it fell over it. It traced the outline of the creature enough so Leo could pull out an ornate short sword and slash at it. There was a high pitch squeal, as the silver blade connected with it, and a thick black ooze began to seep from what seemed thin air.

Seemingly from the shock, the thing let go of her and she jerked herself away from it. When she looked backward, she finally was able to see it. It hadn't been thin air. The being she saw caused her to blink to be sure she wasn't seeing things. It wasn't overly tall, and one couldn't really say it was standing. It wasn't floating either. It almost seemed like an overexaggerated jellyfish. It had a cap-like top, as big as a medium sized dog. Dropping down from what she assumed was its body, that were billions of thread-thin tentacles, most holding it up, but some were writhing around its abdomen, almost as if it were swimming in the air. She wasn't able to analyse it any further before Leo tossed the blade he held. It met its target swiftly and directly. There was one last cringe-worthy squeal from the creature, before it dropped and heavily slammed against the floor.

"Come on, let us go." Leo said to her, without even glancing in her direction again. He was noticeably angry, and a part of Hope understood why. However, at the same time, she was in a towel and water was still dripping from her body onto the floor.

"Excuse you, I'm not leaving here in a towel." Even though she understood why he was frustrated with her, her tone flipped it back on him, as if he had been the one in the wrong. When she spoke, his eyes snapped back to her, his expression shifting for a split second. The look on his face said that he'd gotten a good look at her this time, finally seeming to have noticed that she was attractive in his eyes. It was the first time she'd actually seen this kind of stare from him. She'd somewhat seen it in Sam, but then he didn't seem to be the type to hide much of anything. Although Leo hadn't really hidden anything from her, it seemed that he simply hadn't truly noticed her as a man notices a woman, until now. Currently, in the state she was in, it would be hard not to.

"Uh..." He started, seeming to try to sort through things in his head, very distracted at the moment. "Fine. Get dressed and then we will go. Hurry, Elementum Aquae rarely travel alone." His eyes had seemed to take in every detail of her form, however his mood changed when he saw the symbols near her collar bone and once again, he was angry. Hope made her way toward her bedroom and through the doorway. However, as she was beginning to close the door, he lifted a hand to stop her.

"Do not close it, I cannot protect you if you are behind closed doors." Leo's voice was once again gruff, the tone he frequently used when speaking to her.

"I'm supposed to dress right here in front of you? I don't think so, buddy." She narrowed her eyes at him, as if for a moment, she saw the man in him instead of the scholar. He rolled his eyes at her.

"I will turn away; it is not as if you are in possession of anything I have not seen before." From the tone he used, made it seem as if he meant more than just her nudity. She could tell he had seen the marks and he was not happy about it. Though, there wasn't anything she could do about it right now. He was silent as she quickly slipped her clothes on. He kept his back to her as he had promised. In her hurried state, she'd completely forgotten about the mirror on the wall opposite of her, which allowed Leo semi-unintentional glances as she moved about. He hadn't intended to do so, but he was basically human, after all. A part of him was still powerless to resist the pull of natural, carnal urges.

After dressing, she began to pile things onto the bed that she wanted to take with her, to which Leo turned and almost growled to her.

"What are you doing now?" His voice was impatient. "We do not have time for you to pack up your household. We must be going before others come. This was a sign that they are hunting you now. You have not made a choice and they will force your hand...both sides."

Hope stopped, putting her hands on her hips and scowling at him once again.

"I'm not going back to a dirty and disgusting trailer again unless I have some things of my own with me. You forget that *I* didn't sign on for this, I had no choice." It was very clear to Leo that she didn't intend to budge on this subject and after a brief scoff, he softened a bit.

"Fine. Only what you absolutely need and then we go." Leo sighed, he could tell that she was going to give him grief at every turn, which both frustrated and intrigued him. He wasn't used to anyone standing up to him. In fact, he wasn't used to other people in general. He didn't have much to do with the outside world, except for the infrequent casual conversation of normal spontaneous interactions. He hadn't had to worry about pleasing anyone else or taking care of anyone else, not since his last charge.

Henry David. The name of the last *Talyâ d'Alâhâ* was Henry David. Over the many years while Leo had taught him, protected him, and counselled him they had become companions. To an extent, they had almost become friends. Though, they had never gotten as close as they could have been. If Leo had gotten close to every person under his charge, he would have had a lot of heartache over the course of time, a part of him was still human, after all. Time and semi-immortality did not take that away, it just built walls. He remembered every one, in great detail, but had only gotten close enough to miss them with vague remembrance. One of the many reasons, he craved to be finished with this world and this job.

"Catch." Hope said, pulling him out of his thoughts, in time to have the wind knocked from him, as he caught the heavy bag she'd thrown at him. She winced with how hard it had hit him, but quickly recovered her poise, turning away to call her cat. "Kitty-kitty-kitty!" She called, the words flowing so quickly off her tongue that they blended together. Set was nowhere to be found. She moved to a kitchen cabinet, pulling a can of wet cat food out of it. As she pulled the top and it made the crisp sound of the airlock being broken, as if by magic, the cat appeared and began crying as if he were starving to death. Hope scooped it out into a bowl and placed it onto the floor for him.

"Absolutely not," Leo shook his head emphatically. "Let it go outside or give it away, I do not care what you do with it, but it is not going with us." To which Set paused his feast, just long enough to look up at him with arrogant disapproval.

"If Set doesn't go, I don't go." Hope crossed her arms over her chest in defiance. "Besides, what do you care? It's not like he could make much more of a mess at your house than it already is." She tapped her foot on the floor a few times.

"You have not been to my home." Leo lofted the bag over his shoulder, walking toward the door. "Bring the damn cat, I do not wish to argue with you, there are much more pressing issues at hand. We do not have time to bicker about inconsequential nonsense."

"What do you mean, I've not been to your home? I was just there before I came here?" Hope plucked Set up off of the floor, holding him tightly as he struggled to get back to his bowl of food. She was confused. If that wasn't where he lived, why did he have a room there? It was obvious that he spent a lot of his time at the trailer, could it be possible that the trailer was just storage or a research location? Maybe it was a hide out to get away from danger? Again, so many questions. Why didn't he keep his work in his home like a normal person? Speaking of work, what was she going to do about her job? Her home had been compromised, she could tell by the way Leo had behaved and what he'd said about taking her home previously, that she wouldn't be able to come back to this place. Still holding onto her cat, she glanced around when she reached the door. Silently she said her goodbyes to her old world, so that she could jump feet first into the new one. She would miss her old life and the monotony of the day to day, but she also felt the pull and responsibility of this new chapter. She slowly closed the door behind her and stepped into the role that she'd been born for.

Hope plopped into the passenger seat of Leo's unimpressive vehicle, letting Set free to explore after she had closed the door. The cat seemed to still be a little tiffed with her about having been gone, but for the time being he was preoccupied with examining the new environment he'd been introduced to. Hope on the other hand, stared straight ahead, filtering through the thoughts swirling around in her head. Without even glancing toward her, Leo started the car and began driving toward an unknown destination.

"How did you get to my apartment without the car?" She piped up after a few moments.

"I called in a favor." Leo replied without looking in her direction.

"A favor?" She repeated him, not truly interested, more making conversation than anything.

"Yes, a favor." That annoyed emphasis that he often had about repeating himself seeped from his words like a thick syrup, but he said nothing more about it. Instead, he threw out an accusation. "I see you let Sam convince you to be marked. When did it happen that you and he became so close?" It seemed that he had dwelled on the thought for so long that it just came pouring out of him, almost unconsciously.

"Convinced?!" She shot back at him, misplaced anger directed toward Leo. "I didn't have a choice in the situation, but at least he cares enough to try to be proactive about protecting me! Unlike you, who rarely even notices whether I am around or not!" She leaned her whole body away from him in the car and once again crossed her arms over her chest in somewhat of a pout. Leo huffed, as she once again turned his frustrations back on him, as if any of it was truly his fault. It seemed that if she was very good at getting out of situations by turning the focus on the faults of others. It was clear to him that he was going to have to try a new approach with this one, considering his normal tactics had been failing miserably. Once again, his appearance softened.

"Just be mindful…" He mentioned. "…some things in this world, you do not want to see." He glanced in her direction, noticing that her entire visage had stiffened like an angry porcupine. He let the issue go for a few more moments, before he added to it. "It is not that I do not care. It is that I cannot care." His words were soft, and he wasn't sure that he'd ever actually spoke that thought to anyone before. It wasn't that he hadn't felt it, it was more that he was guarded enough not to want anyone to know it. The vulnerability in his voice caused Hope to look at him, watch him, as she had done several times before, in the last few days. However, this time something had changed in him. He was thoughtful, as he always was, but there was also a sadness in him that she couldn't deny that was brought to her own attention.

"Why?" The single word caught him from his thoughts and caused him to bring his full attention to her, meeting her own stare so much so that he almost couldn't pull his attention away. This distraction caused the car to swerve and brought him from where his thoughts had wandered. Which was a good thing, because when his mind gathered his thoughts together, it made him a bit nervous. His re-action, when he allowed his mind to be consumed by her, was troubling. It wasn't the kind of magic that he was used to, it was a far more ancient force. A force he'd experienced similarly once in his long life. He shook it off, switching gears back to a more professional attitude. He would probably need to eventually address how he felt around her, but not at this moment. Currently, he was steering a metal death trap along a winding road. He focused on that and pretended she wasn't beside him.

Morning was beginning to break by the time Leo once again put the car into park. The sun had crept into the sky just enough to paint the building in front of them in a golden glow. Shock graced Hope's face as she stared forward, mouth agape at the sight of it. Leo left the keys in the car when he got out and made his way toward the house. It was a manor style home, like something out of a fairy-tale. It was far removed from the trailer she'd been to before. Leo didn't pay her much attention when they arrived, but she was beginning to get used to it. What she didn't know was that his aversion was for completely different reasons than they had been before.

"This is your home?" She called after him, her question rhetorical, the kind of question she realized after having already said it, that he would likely be annoyed with. "Why in the Hell would you want to work in that crappy trailer, when you have this?"

"Many reasons, most of all it eliminates distraction." He made the mistake of looking toward her, as he let her in the unlocked door. "It...uh...this place...has other purposes." He tore his eyes from her and continued inside. Hope was puzzled as to why his behavior seemed to have changed so drastically within the last few hours. He hadn't seemed that way while they were at her apartment. He was odd to begin with, so she decided not to overthink it. "Make yourself at home, I will return shortly." He disappeared into the large house, before she could even put Set down. The cat skittered off almost as quickly as Leo had. She wasn't concerned about Set getting lost, but moreso for herself in this large castle-esque structure. He would reappear again when he was hungry.

After several moments of finding several locked doors, Leo came sauntering toward her. He seemed calmer and his hair was dripping. He had changed clothes; his attire was much more casual than what he'd been wearing before. He almost looked normal and while she had her fill of looking him over, he very obviously was looking everywhere except in Hope's direction. The man had something about him, an attractiveness, unlike Sam's rugged, cowboy handsome appearance. Now that Hope was able to actually see more than just an arrogant, geek, there was something about him beyond the appearance, beyond the intelligence, she couldn't quite put a finger on it, but there was something there that she hadn't noticed before.

"Is this where I'm supposed to stay? Or am I to stay at the trailer? Why didn't you bring me here first?" There it was, her plethora of questions, which caused Leo to snap out of the awkward silence he had allowed between them. He shoved his hands into his pant pockets, before moving in the opposite direction of her.

"Come with me." He spoke to her, not answering any of her questions really, outwardly annoyed with her. He had left his previous thoughts behind, replacing them with his natural state of asshole. Hope followed him, whereas she wasn't really sure what was where in this rather large 'house'. He made his way up the stairs and toward one of many rooms on the second floor. "You can put your things in here, as long as you stay in this house, you may call this room your own. You are welcome to go anywhere you like, I merely ask that the locked doors remain locked and unless I allow you inside of them, you stay clear."

Hope looked around the room he'd offered her. It was almost as big as her apartment and had an en-suite. Clearly, he was trying to make her feel as much at home as possible, even though it would never quite be the same, she did appreciate the attempt. She put her things down and looked back at him. "Thank you." She paused for a few moments, then as he was beginning to leave, she piped up. "I'm going to need a few things. I didn't have a chance to grab everything that I will need going forward." She was very matter of fact about it, but only received a confused expression from Leo. "Set needs supplies...and so do I." The way she had said it made it obvious what she was talking about, and a sudden realization seemed to come over him.

"Right." He paused for a moment. "You are not to use your accounts; I will take care of it."

"I'm a big girl, I can take care of myself." Defiance spread over her face, and she crossed her arms over her chest.

"I am sure you can, but you are not going anywhere without an escort. This home is warded against all forces, both good and evil. Neither side can enter or see without permission. Not even Sam or Yhidrial have access here. The only being in all of existence that might supersede that protection is God, himself." Leo crossed his arms over his chest looking off toward the door as if he almost expected a knock. "I would not know; I have never met the man...but it would make sense that He who created everything would not be required to follow such rulings." He looked back toward her, no longer seeming to be as distracted as he had been earlier.

"Fine." Hope rolled her eyes and took her bag into the room, tossing it down onto the bed, before once again studying the room. It would do, she decided.

"I will send someone up with currency. You may go any time you like. There is a garage just behind the house. You may borrow a vehicle. You should be back before dark. I will be here. I have work to do." He wasn't going to be as busy as he seemed to imply, but he wanted to avoid being around her any more than he had to, at least until he gained a handle on the thoughts and emotions he had been having. "Oh...and one more thing. Keep watch for threats, they will be after you. Now that you have the markings of Caelum et Infernum , you might as well use them. Any other repercussions, side effects, and benefits we shall delve into later. For now, I have work to do."

After what seemed forever, there came a knock on the door frame. Hope answered to see a young woman. She seemed to be around the age of 16 to the naked eye. However, with her new sight, she could see looming around her, like the shadow of a ghost, a color tinted halo. Hope was still getting used to this new ability, but she had started to recognize the differences between natural and unnatural soul auras. She'd heard theories of the meanings of auras, but she was beginning to get the idea that the accuracy of those theories left a bit to be desired. The aura of this girl was a pale yellow, much like Da Vinci's, except the girl's was a slightly darker shade and it seemed to almost sparkle with energy. This was the only way Hope could truly describe it. It was almost as if her aura was charged with static electricity. Thankfully, Hope had chosen to wear a sweater that blocked the light of the symbols on her chest as she supernaturally sized the girl up.

"Beannachtaí. An bhfuil tú réidh, leanbh Dé ?" The girl began speaking in a language Hope did not know and if this were any normal situation, she would not have understood the girl's words. Today, however, she *did* understand, but for some reason, her instincts told her to keep this her gift to herself as much as possible, for the time being. So, she responded with a questioning gaze. The emotion she portrayed was not faked, she truly was curious about the girl, who she was, and what her story might have been. "Beg pardon, misses." The girl seemed almost embarrassed that she had used the foreign language, at first. *Her* accent was Irish or Scottish in nature, though slightly off from anything Hope had ever heard before. Silently, Hope wondered why it was that every person she'd met in the past few days seemed to be from different parts of the world, none seeming to speak English as a first language. Then again, she supposed that when one lives for as long as Leo and Sam, one might make friends with many different types of people. "I sometime forget some dunno the words I say." Leo and Sam certainly seemed to be much more fluent with the English language than this girl.

"It's alright." Hope smiled at her warmly. Even

though she was not ready to trust the girl, just being around her seemed to bring out fond feelings. Hope wondered if that was simply because she seemed like a young girl, her friendly demeanor, or maybe it was something the girl was doing to her. In the last couple of days, she had come to expect the un-expected. At this point, 'normal' might have actually shocked her more.

"You in ready go?" The girl asked her. Hope had to catch herself a few times wanting to correct the girl. She was still trying to figure the woman out and until she did, she was going to be sure not to offend her. "Maestro given…" The girl paused to search through her mind for words, when she couldn't find them, she reached into the large purse she held on her shoulder. When she pulled her hand from the purse, it held a stack of $50 dollar bills so large that she could barely stretch her fingers around it.

Hope was absolutely shocked, unsure if she had ever seen that amount of cash in person before. She was sure she hadn't.

"Is that all for me?" It was rhetorical, but the girl seemed as if she didn't understand that Hope didn't need an answer to the question. She knew the purpose of the money was to make her feel more at home here and possibly an apology for the several times that Leo had been arrogant, self-righteous, and rude to her.

"Tá." The girl spoke while nodding her head. "M'ainm is Venetia, I help while you here." Hope nodded to the girl, turning back into the room to grab her purse. She fidgeted with the glass ring on her finger a bit as she walked behind the girl leading her outside. She might never need to use it, but she wouldn't be without it again, not after the incident with the floating jellyfish monster.

Venetia brought her to a large garage behind the house. It was also unlocked, as the house had been, and when Venetia flipped on the lights, Hope's eyes went wide. The collection of vehicles was astounding. As she walked into the garage, she saw mint condition cars that ranged from the earliest known to some obviously produced within the last few years. It would seem that when something struck his liking, he made it his own. When she had met him, she would have never guessed he owned the things he did. She couldn't fathom why he'd shown her the trailer first and not brought her here. After a few moments, Hope realized that she had been walking alone and looked back toward Venetia. She seemed to be waiting, before she proceeded further.

"You choose, we go." Venetia spoke, as she watched the other woman intently. Hope wasn't sure which to choose, so she just made a decision based on the car she was standing by at the time. It was an electric blue, 1977 Pontiac Firebird , with t-tops, black interior, and a black bird symbol emblazoned with light blue flames over the hood. The car truly was a sight of beauty, and she was more than satisfied with her choice.

"This one." Hope said to the girl, who in response, made her way toward the passenger side of the vehicle.

"Good." The girl spoke, getting into the car, obviously expecting Hope to drive. Hope was confused. She had assumed the girl would drive, considering she seemed to be working for Da Vinci. She had also assumed that the keys were in the vehicle, considering she hadn't seen the girl grabbing any before they got into the car. Hope slipped into the driver's seat, moving her hands over the steering wheel in a gentle caress. She then turned to the girl, reaching out her hand. The girl responded with a confused expression.

"Keys?" Hope asked her. The girl, in response, didn't speak a word. She just smiled and reached over to the dash behind the wheel. She pressed a button that Hope would not have seen unless she had been shown. Immediately after the button was pressed, the car roared to life. Hope was again impressed. Hope had heard how much ingenuity and intelligence Leo had possessed in the history books she had read, but the books paled in comparison to the truth. They paled in comparison to her current opinion of him. He was frustrating, almost infuriating, but the real man was quite an enigma. She carefully pulled the classic car out of the garage and set off in the direction that Venetia pointed her in. Her energy was renewed at the thought of a full day of shopping with the large stack of bills that she'd been shown, with very few limits. It was exciting, considering Hope had never felt so limitless in her life. The confines of human potential, Sam had given her an extension to. The budget of her financial status, Leo had assisted with. For the moment, she almost forgot about the war she had been forced into. She almost forgot about choosing a side. For now, even her suspicions of her shopping companion had faded slightly. Her intention was to load up with caffeine, grab some sort of breakfast, and shop until she literally dropped, unable to keep going any longer.

5

Hope tossed the last few bags into the back seat of the car. The trunk had already been loaded so full that it would barely close, and the back seat was nearly covered, as well. Hope had somewhat gotten to know Venetia throughout the day. She knew that her shopping companion, like Leo, was much older than she appeared. The girl was Druidic, which was why her aura glittered. Hope still kept the sight to herself, acting surprised when Venetia had told her that she wasn't completely human anymore. At one time she had been, but long ago her people had made her into what she was and with that new life she had left her mortality behind. She didn't remember how old she was anymore; she didn't count how many years passed by any longer.

As Hope slipped back into the driver's seat of the Firebird, she held a large smile on her face, not only because of the giant haul that she had just purchased, but because she was feeling like she might have made an actual friend in her world as it was now. Venetia didn't seem to be someone that was forced to protect her or someone who needed anything from her. True, she worked for Leo, and he had told the girl to go with her, but Venetia hadn't been forced to be casual or friendly with her. That was something that Hope felt as if she had earned. It was in that moment that she turned her gaze to the girl beside her. However, the look on the girl's face wasn't what she had assumed she would see.

"You are not what expected." Venetia began, a blank sadness suddenly set in the features of her face. "They say you break balance. Can not have that, see?" The girl looked into her eyes and there was a softness in them. Hope tensed up when the girl started speaking but was once again lulled by a comfort similar to when they had first met. That couldn't have been a coincidence and so she fought it with everything she had now, trying to keep away from direct eye contact. Venetia pulled out a decorated dagger, an object that looked as if it had fallen directly out of the Holy Roman Empire. She held it there for a moment, staring forward. "I sorry, but we can not risk. Slán, ba bhreá liom bualadh leat. "

The loose translation her new gift gave her said that it was time to get out of the car, which took Hope only seconds to accomplish. When she was out of the vehicle, she scrambled to her feet holding tight to the glass ring and shouting as loud as she could. A single name echoed through the parking garage as if she were standing in the Grand Canyon. "SAMAEL!" The name seemed to startle the other girl for a moment, but then she shook her head, a small smile forming over her lips.

"Not to help you." Her words were whispered as she slowly made her way out of the vehicle. "Asmodeus is not allow." Hope blinked, beginning to be nervous that she might be right. Sam had not appeared, and the glass ring sat dormant on her finger. She took a few deep, nervous breaths, trying to calm herself. Venetia's eyes began to light up a deep yellow, as if a fire were building deep inside of her. As her internal light began to grow brighter, symbols over every bit of exposed skin revealed themselves to Hope. Distracted by the writing on the girl's body, Hope hadn't noticed the brightness built up within her empty hand, it became so bright that it lit up the entire parking lot.

Quick thinking and pure luck landed Hope on her ass, as she jumped away from it, when the energy ball was thrown in her direction. It sizzled through the air as it whirred past her and exploded with extreme force against a back wall of the parking garage. A few electric charges hit nearby vehicles and scoured them with black marks. She assessed the situation, trying to figure out what she could use to her benefit. Ultimately, Venetia was human, an extended lifespan and perpetual youth, but not completely immortal. Before her opponent could build up another magical nuke to use against her, Hope jumped into the Firebird shoving her finger against the button, to which the car responded. In Hope's heightened state of emotion, something happened to the car and the inside of it lit up, as if she had turned the interior lights on, but their bulbs remained dark. The headlights lit up on their own and seemed brighter than they originally were. It seemed to catch Venetia off guard and instead of growing brighter, the energy ball she had built up faltered a bit. Hope shifted the car into gear, holding her foot on the break, her eyes intent on the startled woman standing in front of the car.

"Nice to meet you..." Hope spoke, loud enough for the

girl to hear her, her tone gaining strength as she finished her sentence. "...bitch!" With her last word, she slammed her foot on the gas, plowing straight through the Druid, into the cement wall in front of her. The crunch of bone and metal rang through the entire enclosure. Energy poured from Hope, through the car, and into the girl. The impact of the car was magically enhanced, providing the necessary blow to neutralize the enemy. l Hope was jolted backward in her seat. Her eyes snapped upward, her instincts making sure the girl was no longer a threat. They were met by the gruesome scene she had expected. She had hit her target head on, and the girl had likely been killed almost instantly, a spatter of blood and spit, coughed up by the girl shortly after, glistening in the lights, which were now once again back to a much dimmer normalcy. A wave of fear pulsed through Hope, knowing that something in her had made this much worse than it should have been. She couldn't worry about that now. She needed to get away before anyone came along and started asking questions.

Hope took a few deep breaths, pulling the car back a few feet, before getting out to look over the damage. The car itself was a tank, as it seemed. The damage to the front end was minimal, considering how bad it could have been. She had apparently made a good decision.

"Ya dunna thin' ya can do it on ya own, huh?" A voice came from the passenger side of the vehicle. A voice she recognized, from a person that she was not exactly happy with at the moment.

"Where were you!?" She shouted at him. Angerly, she stomped toward the passenger side of the car, and threw open the door. She put her hands on her hips as she stared at Sam, who had shown up after she'd already taken care of matters herself. "You said to call if I needed you. I needed you, where were you!?"

"With ya, eva bit of a way." He snapped his fingers and the blood disappeared from the front end of the car; however, the damage was still there, and the mess of Venetia still crumpled up on the ground. "Betta get outta 'ere, ya show gots some attention. I got a cameras. 'Til lata, Deifilia." With that, he disappeared again. Hope could hear the sound of sirens in the background. He was right, she had to get out of here, she would have a more detailed conversation with him later. Until then, there were much more important things on her mind. He was gone for now, but she was sure he would show back up eventually. She needed to get back to the chateau and speak to Leo. She was unsure whether he had known there was a traitor in his midst, but she intended to let him know as soon as she got back. Whether he did or did not know, she intended to have a few words with him about the whole situation, and to also gain an understanding of who exactly Asmodeus was and why Sam had not come to help when she called.

It took her a while longer than she had expected to get back to Leo, she had left during the daytime and it had since gotten dark. Everything always looked different in the dark and though she remembered the general direction, Venetia had been there to direct her the last time. She parked the car out front, behind the beater that Leo had been traveling in. She left her purchases behind as she stormed into the house.

She paused only for a moment to listen for which direction she might find Leo in. It didn't take long to hear the creaking of old floorboards and quiet curses of Da Vinci likely at her cat. After all, he hadn't wanted Set here in the first place. She made her way up to where she thought Leo was, thrusting open the door.

"Did you know!?" Hope shouted to him, finding him in a room that looked as if it were decorated in the same style of chaos as the trailer had been.

"Hm?" Leo looked up from the book he was focused on questioningly.

"Venetia, did you know she was working against us?" Hope continued with the same loud tone.

"I had suspicions." Calmly, he went back to what he had been doing, as if there was nothing wrong and Hope wasn't furious. This action only made her more angry and almost shocked at his nerve to freely admit this to her.

"And you didn't even care to let me know? Or send me with any kind of protection? Or help at all?" She was so upset that she was shaking. Fuming, she charged over to the desk, swiping a hand across it and knocking everything in front of him onto the floor. Leo let out something of a growl, before his hands folded into tight fists, slowly allowing his eyes to move up to meet hers.

"You survived." His tone was fierce, Hope could tell that she had actually angered him now, instead of merely annoying him. She felt justified. He had known that she could have been in danger, and he hadn't even had the respect to let her know about it.

"You're an asshole." She sneered at him, standing there

staring at him as he stood and moved around the desk to face her.

"Astute observation. Would you like to state anything else blatantly obvious or are you finished with your assertions?" He narrowed his eyes at her, looking down into her eyes, his own filling with rage and something she couldn't quite put her finger on.

"You could have at least let me know!" She still shouted, even though he was close enough to her that she didn't have to.

"I could have. I didn't." He said, his voice filled with the same emotions that his eyes still held, staring at her as if he was unable to remove them.

"You're supposed to protect me! How can you protect someone that you refuse to even be around?!" She knew the question was rhetorical before she had even let it leave her lips. However, to her pure astoundment, it wasn't ill-tempered words he replied with.

Instead, Leo grabbed her by the arm, pulling her close, and pressed a forceful kiss to her lips. She had been so startled by the action that she hadn't even had time to resist it and by the time she realized what was going on, her instincts wouldn't let her. On the contrary, she settled into the kiss, which deepened, and his grip loosened. He dropped his grasp, both hands moving to meet in the middle of her back, pulling her closer to him. For the next few moments, they were not Leonardo Da Vinci and Hope Brenner. They were not The Architect and The Chosen. They were just a man and a woman, in an embrace, the whole world melting around them.

Unfortunately, it was an experience that didn't last. He

pulled away abruptly, turning his back on her, and walking away. Hope was left standing there, not truly knowing how to react to what had just happened. She was speechless.

"That is why. It was easier to let you walk into danger than it was to face what was building within myself." Without anything further being said, he left the room and Hope with it. She hadn't considered him in such a way, with the exception of a small peak of interest earlier that day. She certainly hadn't considered that it might be the reason why he'd behaved the way he did. She had thought it was something to do with the symbols, now permanently embellished on her body. After a short while of being alone in the room, thinking to herself, she came back to her senses and glanced around. Now that her anger and the shock of everything that had happened that day had subsided, she was able to take in more of the room and she remembered everything she had left in the vehicle. It didn't take long for her to make her way back to where she had parked the car, however it wasn't there any longer and Leo was nowhere to be found.

Upon getting back to the room he had given her, she saw everything she had purchased today was already there, the bags piled around the room, as if it had been moved there quickly and left behind in disarray. She pulled the litter box she'd purchased out of one of the bags, quickly filling it with cat litter and opening a can of wet cat food. She poured it into a matching bowl. Instantly, as if by magic, Set danced his way into the room. It was amazing, his uncanny ability to hear a can of cat food opening, and instantly appear, apparently even in the largest of places. Without so much as even truly acknowledging that he had come in, she closed the door behind him. After taking a few pieces of clothing out of her newly acquired bounty, she made her way to the attached bathroom. She needed some quiet time to herself, then she needed some sleep. She intended on trying to clear her mind and relax, but with everything that had happened, she seriously doubted it was a great possibility.

Hope woke up to the snoring of her cat, who had made himself at home, sleeping sprawled out her face. She groaned and pushed him off of her, his only response was a quick stretch and he resettled into the blanket beside her. She stared up at the ceiling for a while, before she actually got up. Everything that had happened in the last couple of days seemed so surreal. Angels, monsters, magic, she assumed demons were real, though she had yet to actually meet one. She now had magical tattoos and a fallen angel protector, of sorts. She was still a bit perturbed with Sam's flakiness when it came to asking him for help. She assumed it had something to do with the person that Venetia had spoken of, Asmodeus. Sam and Leo had spoken to him before also. Leonardo Di Vinci had kissed her...the thought crossed her mind nonchalantly at first, but then her thoughts came to a screeching halt. She went back to the thought, replaying last night over in her head. She replayed it so many times that she could almost feel the moment again. She still wasn't sure how she wanted to feel about it, whether she wanted to be mad at him about it or not. She hoped it wouldn't be awkward now. Finally, she got out of bed, ran a brush through her hair, then tied it up in a messy bun with a scrunchie. She wasn't ready to get dressed yet, but she was getting hungry. She also still had an unsatisfied curiosity about the house and its contents.

Barefoot, she made her way toward where she had found the kitchen yesterday, as quietly as she could. However, to her surprise, the kitchen wasn't there. She glanced around confused, trying to figure out what had happened to the kitchen or if she had made a wrong turn. She was suddenly *very* confused.

"Stealth, as it seems, is not a gift of yours." A voice came from behind her. It made her stiffen, then turn slowly. Hope offered Leo an awkward smile. He had broken the silence, but she didn't know how to act around him now. His appearance was again very casual, and he showed no signs of embarrassment or shyness, in fact, he acted as if nothing had happened at all. It made Hope feel odd, and it made her question whether it had even happened at all, maybe she had dreamed it?

"I just... I can't find the kitchen." Hope spoke in a calm and quizzical voice. Leo only replied with a shrug.

"Understandable, considering it is not always in the same place." This statement only confused Hope more.

'Isn't always in the same place?' She thought it to herself, knowing that repeating the man would only annoy him. "Where else would it be?" She asked, unsure how logically a whole room could just be somewhere else within a day. Leo smiled at her.

"Now, that is a question, is it not?" He began walking away from her, putting his hands in his pockets. She wasn't sure if he wanted her to follow him, but she did anyway. He answered her unspoken question after a short distance, when he began to speak to her again. "Surely you did not think that I would retire from the practice of creation, innovation, and the search for the unknown after going underground?"

Somehow, out of the thousands of tiles on the floor of the entryway, he put pressure on a specific one and the house began to groan. He reached out to grab her and pull her away from the place she was standing as the floor slowly began to twist and rise in the center of the room. She heard the gears and metallic movement only moments before. When the movement finally stopped, in front of them stood something that looked like an elevator but seemed as if it had been constructed long before it *should* have been possible. She watched as Leo made his way into the small structure.

"Do not be concerned, it has a capacity of up to six hundred pounds. Tried and tested." He spoke to her as she made her way inside. If she understood correctly, he had just told her that this little room had held six hundred pounds worth of *something* in it at one time. "Stay near the back, we would not want you to lose an appendage." He pulled a lever, and the elevator began to move downward. As it seemed, each notch represented a level and he had to do so one at a time. It wasn't like the elevators that she knew, but nonetheless it was still impressive. When they hit the bottom level, the opening that they had come in was facing a steel wall. Leo pulled the lever outward and pushed it to the right. As he did so, Hope jumped, because the sheet of metal behind her slid forcefully open and instantly the elevator was filled brilliance.

When the girl could finally see again, her eyes adjusted

to the brightness of the room, she saw a machine. It was beautiful. Golden rings and moving parts lit up by symbols, sparkling and awe inspiring. She stared at it. Watching it, she was almost hypnotized. She had no idea what it did or if it even did anything beyond twist within itself and generate light, but it was amazing.

"A work of art, is it not?" Leo stood back, admiring his work, of which it seemed he might do frequently. "I assure you; its purpose is even more than its beauty. This...is the Centrenarithan ."

"Centra-na what?" Hope tried to repeat him, before she was able to stop herself. Leonardo rolled his eyes and took a deep breath.

"Centrenarithan ." He repeated himself, seeming very annoyed. Not only did she try to repeat him and fail, but he had to repeat himself again in order to correct her. "Do not waste your time trying to remember hearing of it. You do not know anything of this. This is of my own design... if you should require it, there are schematics in the library." He glanced toward her, trying not to let his eyes linger for too long, but noticing that she was still staring at the lettering on the rings. "I am guessing you will not. Though, trying to read the machine while it is running is largely an impossible task."

"...and God said let there be light and there was light..." She read from one of the spinning rings. She didn't have to hide that she could read the Hebrew in front of him. He seemed to be surprised anyway, but not for long. He walked up beside her, before he spoke again, also staring at the moving rings.

"You are the only soul, save myself, that has ever seen this in person...currently living anyway." He kept staring at the machine, even when Hope glanced in his direction. "It must be protected. In our hands it has, will, and could do much good in this world...but in the wrong hands it could cause a lot of destruction." He could feel her eyes on him, so he met her stare. "Yhidrial and Samael do not know it is here, nor will they ever, as far as I am concerned." Hope tried very hard not to allow her eyes to wander over him like an animal assessing their prey. As soon as Leo caught on to the way she was looking at him, he pulled his sight away from her and walked several steps away, pretending to be working on something. It was difficult to maintain such a causal relationship after what had happened between them.

"Why? What's so important about it?" Hope asked, facing the sphere again, filing away her any other thoughts for now.

"The less you know, the better. At least, for the time being." Leo didn't answer her questions, but she knew he wasn't going right now. She had begun to have the ability to judge his moods and currently he seemed very closed off "Also, yes it did. No, I will not. There are many reasons." She had no idea what he was talking about. It seemed he was having a conversation with himself. He rolled his eyes, noticing the bewilderment written in her features. "Yes. Last night did happen. No. I will not let it happen again. There are many reasons." Finally, Hope caught on and nodded in disappointed agreement. She wasn't upset that nothing would happen. In truth, she wasn't even sure if she had wanted anything to happen in the first place. The disappointment was that he shot it down so quickly. He hadn't read her mind or done anything supernatural, as it seemed, he simply had read her non-verbal cues.

"I get it." She replied, even though she really didn't. She just wanted the conversation to be over. He noticed her change in behavior, deciding that he should clarify himself.

"It is not a question of what I want." He took a deep breath. "There are many factors that have to be accounted for. What happened last night was a mistake..." He paused, likely reliving last night in his mind or possibly whatever caused him to come to this decision. "...a favorable lapse in judgement, but it cannot happen again."

'Again...?' Hope thought to herself. 'Did he mean women in general, the kiss, or someone like her? She began to reply but was cut off before she could even get a word out.

"No. No questions. You will stay away from this." Da Vinci circled back to the no questions policy. "You're welcome to anything else that I have, but this..." He looked directly at her, into her eyes. Something was different about him; the same stubbornness was there, but now also a sadness to it. "...this you leave alone."

That said, he walked toward the elevator and stood there waiting for her. She hadn't completely had her fill of the machine, but it could wait. The elevator ride up seemed much longer than the ride down, possibly due to the silence between them. Not another word was said and when they reached the ground level, he remained with her just long enough for her to get out of the elevator, then he tapped the pressure plate tile. Before the elevator even finished sinking into the floor, Leo began to walk away. Hope was curious as to what had happened, but she let it go. Clearly, he was upset. She wasn't sure what had caused it, but something in the conversation had triggered the negative reaction. Beyond what Leo had said, instinct told her to it was neither the time nor the place for this conversation. Leo, once again, disappeared into the large house. He still hadn't told her where the kitchen was and, from the looks of it, he didn't intend to.

She made her way back to her room, deciding to get dressed and venture out into the world to find food. She hadn't spent everything that Leo had given her, far from it, in fact. She stashed some of the cash around the room, keeping plenty in her wallet to go with her when she would eventually leave. Hope showered and dressed quickly, she wasn't in the mood to meet up with 'Sir Buzz Killington' in the hallway and give him the opportunity to tell her she couldn't go. She still had a lot to think about, a lot to figure out. She could answer a lot of questions here if she tried, but this was not where she wanted to be at the moment. She needed air. She hadn't been here for long, but it wasn't the amount of time, it was what that filled that time. She still hadn't completely processed everything. How could she? Hope felt like she was living in a dream or maybe a nightmare, depending on how one perceived the situation. Considering Leo wasn't exactly forthcoming with information, and he obviously didn't want to see her at the moment, she set her sights on pulling information from the only other individual that might possibly be able to answer her questions. Sam.

Almost immediately after she pulled the Firebird out of the driveway, Sam was there. He appeared in a spot very similar to when they first met, reclined in the back seat, feet up on the center console.

"Ya rang, Deifilia?" A lazy voice from the backseat spoke. Hope was expecting him. She hadn't called him, but she was curious as to whether he was only listening for her call or if the ring was more like a constant spy.

"I didn't, but I also knew it was a great possibility you would show up when I left Leo's." She replied, glancing for a brief second in the rear-view mirror. He merely nodded watching the scenery pass by.

"So'uh...where we off to then?" Sam asked, there was no concern in his voice, he seemed to just be making casual conversation.

"Anywhere, but there." She stated under her breath. The vague answer actually seemed to peek Sam's interest more than more direct answers. He sat up and looked straight into the rear-view mirror at her eyes, trying to judge her reactions.

"Ya popped The Architect, din't ya?" From the man's re-action, it seemed this accusation was juicy gossip.

"I did what?" She knew what he was saying, by the way he behaved, but she was going to make him spell it out for her.

"Ya popped 'im. Ya know, hide a stick, ridin' a pony, buryin' a snake, cooked his sausage, poked a panther..." He seemed able to recite every euphemism for 'the deed' since the dawn of time, and so she interrupted him.

"Not that it's any of your business, but no. I didn't." Sam hopped into the front seat, leaning in close enough to, oddly enough, smell her.

"Nope, ya definitely did somethin' wit ol' boy, you reek of guilt, rejection, frustration, and Maestro da Vinci. I could smell it from a ten-mile radius." Now in the front seat, he put his feet up on the dash. "Ya dunna wanna talk about it, s'alright, ya dun 'ave to." Hope rolled her eyes.

"There's nothing to talk about." She shrugged her shoulders. "He kissed me. He decided he didn't want to again. That's all. Nothing more." Sam narrowed his eyes, seeming confused.

"Don't make sense…'cept…" He paused, took a deep breath, then nodded. "It's 'cause a her ." Yet again, without context, she was left with no answers. A part of her wondered if every supernatural entity was as cryptic as those she'd met so far. Sam shrugged. "He's just had a rough life, s'all." He seemed to understand that she must be getting frustrated at having a lot of questions and no one providing any answers. Hope huffed at his sympathy for Leo, rolling her eyes. To which, Sam responded by changing the topic of conversation. "So then, what'cha plan, love? Ya gunna 'ave a night out…a ya gunna get goin' all together?" He asked her, as if she had a choice, something which hadn't been a common theme lately. She looked at him like he'd just asked her if she was about to drive to the moon.

"I don't know…" She paused, glancing over to him quickly, then back at the road. "… I suppose I didn't really think about it in terms of where I was going. I just needed to get away. Sort out my thoughts. Regroup. You know?"

"Regroupin's a good thing a do." That was his only reply, simply lounging in the passenger seat, still reclined, arms across his chest. She supposed he was giving her time to think, but instead it did the opposite. Plus, she was curious in general.

"What do you do when you're not following me and running errands for the mob?" She asked him, tossing him a quick sideways glance.

"Little a this an' a little a that...depends on a decade." He shrugged, looking toward her and letting his eyes linger. "How 'bout ya?" To which, Hope shrugged, keeping her eyes on the road.

"I don't know. It's been so long since I've done anything except for going to work and staying home...now that I don't really have a home and no longer have a normal job, I don't know what to do with myself anymore." She frowned, thinking about her room at Leo's house. It was decent, but it wasn't home, and she couldn't go back to her apartment, not after what had happened last time.

"Settles that then." He seemed to make a decision for her. "Take ya next right." Hope was somewhat curious as to where they were going. As long as she could take her thoughts off of the rest of life, she didn't really care. She kept in mind who Sam was but welcomed his casual nature. He directed them down a few streets and toward an apartment complex, one of which was very similar to how her own had been. Once she'd parked, he got out and made his way inside. When they were through the door, there was a small entryway and a single set of wide stairs. The interior of the building was old but upkept. The décor seemed to be circa 1800's in nature. Hope wondered silently how the owners replaced details that seemed to be the original pieces hundreds of years later, but it wasn't something that she thought about on for long. She followed Sam up four sets of stairs, to the very top floor. By the time they got there, Hope was almost out of breath.

"Why...do you take the...stairs...:" She had to take a few deep breaths. "...when you can just pop yourself in." Her breathing was finally beginning to normalize. She watched him pull a key out of his pocket and unlock the door. She was just making an observation, not assuming anything at this point.

"Lotsa reasons, but I kinda like a simplicity a it." Sam walked into the room, leaving the door open for her to follow. "Is not much, but it suits."

"This is yours?" Hope asked, now assuming that the apartment had to be his. He just nodded, flopping himself on the couch. He tapped his right temple a couple of times, motioning for something.

"Ya 'ave ta remem'ba ta use the sight, doll. Ya don't know what ya don't know, until what ya don't know gets ya block knocked off." Sam told her. As directed, she did so, her eyes and the symbols on her shoulders lit up. When she did so, the entire room shown bright up with hidden words and images. Some blue, some red, some yellow, and last but now least white. The intricate depiction of each symbol was beautiful, just like that of her ring. Something in them seemed very fluid, as if the person that had put them there had been writing it consistently for a very long time. She could read them, but had she not had the sight, they would have seemed to be beautiful gibberish to her, just like the Italian that Leo's books were in.

"What are they for?" Hope asked, moving to a wall and running her fingers over some of the lines.

"Protection, mostly. A couple a other things, but I tendna think Enochian and Hellspeak topics for a secon' date." Sam answered, laughing under his breath, clearly making a joke, but Hope thought she sensed something more to the comment. "Yeah, it's mine, been so since a building was a wee single story." He made a gesture for small with his thumb and index finger.

"Why the different colors?" Hope was still tracing the lines she saw, soon noticing they were on the floor, ceiling, and doors as well.

"I dunno what Leo told ya, but each a them is a ward. Bit ironic that magic can keep magic out. Is His rules...we all jus' work here." He motioned upward. "Red's a damned. Blue's a blessed. Yella human...then us an' some others, white." Hope looked back toward him, outwardly perplexed.

"Why are we white? Shouldn't you be blue...or red, I guess...and myself yellow?" Her question seemed to be logical conclusion.

"We're white, 'cause is a category made up a those without one." Sam shrugged. "Me, 'cause I ain't got no home. A forsaken ain't automatically evil. An' I ain't allowed in wit a angels. I'm not quite sure 'bout after ya choose yet. is usually white 'til they choose. Not quite sure if givin' ya the sight might'a changed it. Weren't really human ta begin with an' 'cause a the Caelum et Infernum, means ya can't really be one side or the otha. What'cha might call 'true neutral', I suppose." She could tell he was being honest. It seemed as if, even though sometimes Sam didn't tell her things and he manipulated what he said to her, he had never truly lied to her. She blinked a couple of times, allowing her vision to fade back down to normal.

"Others? What others?" Hope knew there were angels and demons, humans and Druids, but what else was there? Sam took a deep breath.

"Lotsa thin's. Ya wouldn't 'ave been able to see 'em 'til now, ya'll learn a person's soul ain't always seem on a outside. Now ya will see 'em, but blessing an' a curse, right? Then ya got 'em like me, made white. Stripped by one side or the other. Both sides got rejects. " Sam nodded. "Creatures's always been neutral, since the beginning an' they ain't in a war, 'cause they didn't get a fair shake ta begin with. World was never theirs, will never be theirs. Kinda a raw deal, if ya ask me." He stopped, adjusted himself on the couch, and changed the subject. "Come on up, Deifilia." He patted the seat next to him. She could have refused, but he didn't think she would. He knew she was still frustrated with him, but the amount of irritation she felt toward him at the moment paled in comparison to what she felt for Leonardo right now. Human females, as intriguing as some were, also held an equal amount of trouble. She got up off of the floor and sat down beside him on the couch. He watched her for a bit, long enough to make her aware and feel awkward.

"What?" Her immediate reaction was defensive. Then, there it was, that crooked grin of his. She shook her head, then rolled her eyes.

"Oh come off it, lass. Can't 'elp a guy for gettin' twitterpated. Seems ya 'ave a way 'bout ya." He kept his eyes on her, his smile never leaving his face. He had to admit, now that Da Vinci had placed a clear boundary with the girl, a part of him wanted to make a play. However, he also couldn't be sure that the desire for her that he felt might be because a part of his soul, or the angelic equivalent, was merged with her own. He had never performed the spell before, so he had no idea what to expect. Ultimately, he pushed thoughts of propriety out of his mind. He wasn't completely oblivious to the humorous irony of the whole situation, the jokes he could make about it. Sam also wasn't sure if she would find it as funny as he did, especially considering he had burdened her with the marks without her permission. "So, what's ya pleasure?"

"What do you mean?" She asked, her cheeks starting to become a flushed shade of pink. Sam snickered to himself, as she made it painfully clear where her thoughts were after his previous comments.

"Movie, sweets. What kind a movie ya like?" As he clarified, she loosened up a bit, taking a deep breath.

"It doesn't matter, anything is fine." Hope leaned back against the couch. She didn't move any closer, but she settled in, trying to be comfortable in what felt like an impossible situation. She knew she should keep her guard up, but Sam seemed so much closer to normal than Leo, it would have been easy to forget what and who he was. Sam stood up, walked over to the television, and flipped it on. A part of her wondered why he didn't use a remote, because once the TV was on, he sat back down on the couch beside her.

"I am McLovin." Sam let out a breath of a laugh and picked up the remote from the end table beside him. It took him mere moments to search for the movie he was looking for. She did say that it didn't matter and what could be better than an R rated comedy, with plenty of dick jokes to make the situation even more awkward, especially watching such a thing with an ex-angel.

"Really? Superbad?" She ran the palm of her hand over her face, before looking at him as if he were completely ridiculous. There it was again, taking advantage of the situation, not deceiving, not lying, but manipulating the situation to suit him. He knew that this movie would likely cause the weird situation to grow and possibly get them both to think inappropriate thoughts. She was suspicious of his intentions. She wasn't even sure of her own intentions, at this point. She had come willingly, knowing that she was going to be alone with him. She knew that with the rejection she experienced this morning her emotions were raw and malleable. She finally decided to give in. She was up for Netflix and chill. She might have even been up for other things, depending on how the day went. A part of her was curious as to what it would be like to be with an angel. Were they anatomically the same as a human? Could someone feel the power they possessed during such an act? She was staring at the TV, but she wasn't watching it. Her videographic mind was watching a movie of its own creation and it was much more risqué than the film could ever be. As if she had been speaking the words in her head out loud, Sam leaned closer, placing a hand to her face, and guiding her to look at him. Once his eyes connected with hers, he spoke to her.

"Not sure if it's a magic I gave ya or a disconnec' with Da Vinci or if it's somethin' else, but I know what you're thinkin'..." Sam eased his way into her personal space and kissed her. It wasn't like kissing Leo. Sam's kiss was warm and determined. She allowed it, in fact, she leaned into it, reaching her hand out to him. The fresh markings emitted warmth and desire through her whole body, lighting up the room in a pulsing white light. It wasn't until the kiss ended that she pulled away slowly and saw that the man in front of her also seemed to surge with radiant energy. It was almost impossible to discern which light was hers and which was his. "...there don't have to be no strings. Ya don't 'ave a keep it all in ya head, I'm game a lend a the cause. I been with a 'uman, but not one wit' my marks."

Hope knew that this whole situation was likely a very bad idea, from going home with him, to being alone with him, and the possibility that something might happen between them. However, a part of her didn't care and wanted to throw caution to the wind. In the end, it wasn't even a contest, and she gave in to curiosity and carnal hunger. This time it was she that moved in for the kiss, only hers wasn't as soft and gentle as his had been. Something inside of her bubbled to the surface and she tackled him like a lioness with its prey. The modification of her behavior was far from unwelcome and Sam reciprocated the animalistic nature. It had been a few days in coming, but it seemed as if it had been an inevitable occurrence. Since the first time she had met him; since she rested her head on his shoulder; on into this moment; there had been a spark of something between them.

6

Just as the room began to heat up, there was a knock on the door. Sam pulled away, breathing heavily, and seeming to listen. Hope had not seen him so out of breath and in that moment, she realized she was truly shocked that an angel could actually be out of breath. Before, she had assumed such beings could not become tired or sick, she had assumed angels and demons would likely be as close to immortal as possible, without being God himself. Once Sam realized she was staring at him, catching her breath just as he was, he quickly stood. His demeanor shifted as if he had been caught with his 'hand in the cookie jar'. Hope didn't understand his reaction, but didn't have time to consider the situation, before there was again a knock at the door. Sam moved to it quickly and glanced through the peephole. When he saw who was on the other side, he quickly grabbed the handle, and opened the door. Once it was open, a girl walked through, seeming to be very casual and comfortable. She walked in as if she owned the place, seeming to pay Sam very little attention, moving past him and on into the other room. Hope wasn't exactly sure how to react to the situation, especially considering she didn't even seem to notice that Hope was even there. Sam just watched the open doorway, acting as if he were about to say something. The girl just kept walking, Sam didn't have an opportunity to say anything, so he closed his mouth, and remained silent, looking back toward Hope. He gave her a half smile, before directing his words to her once more.

"Hope, that's Ja'hari. " He motioned toward the direction the girl had gone. Hope looked in the direction he pointed, then back toward her host.

"Is she like me? Is she human or is she like you? Or...?" Hope hadn't time to use the sight on the girl, before she had disappeared.

"The answer is no. *She* has excellent hearing, and *she* can speak for herself." A voice came from the other room, before the girl poked around the corner. "*She* also has an excellent sense of smell and from the aroma of this room, it seems like I showed up just in time." She gave Sam a disapproving glare. Though, it wasn't one that a girlfriend would give her boyfriend. It was more the sort of gaze that a best friend would give to him for catching him in a mistake. She sighed, then sauntered back into the room. The girl seemed to feel Hope's eyes on her and as the white light within Hope began to become brighter Ja'hari lifted her index finger toward her. "Eh. Not yet, sweet pea." The girl understood what Hope was doing and motioned for her to stop. "That's rude, girl. You really gotta learn better manners than that." The girl had a New England accent, finally a fellow American. She might not have been just like Hope, but at least they might share a similar culture. "Sam, who is this chick and why is she scanning me with 'the sight'?" The girl seemed fairly close to Hope's age, but of course that was just from her human perspective. When Ja'hari had motioned Hope to stop, she did so as quickly as she could, though she was still getting the hang of it. Hope had caught the faint white aura, so she knew that was another thing they had in common. The girl was an outsider, just like she and Sam were. Other than that, they had nothing in common. To the human eye, Ja'hari had perfect caramel color skin, the kind most women dream of having. Her eyes were a jade color, emphasized by her al-mond shaped eyes, lined with artistically placed makeup. Her lips were a full, light pink and her black hair rested straight, long, and nestled around her shapely female form. The girl looked almost as if she could have been a statue, except for the stylish modern apparel she wore. Hope's thoughts drifted for a brief moment, to the fact that she really liked the girl's outfit. Classy, but bold.

"This's Hope." Sam spoke simply, but directly. Ja'hari crossed her arms over her chest, still trying to figure out Sam's angle in this situation. She didn't seem to know any-thing about Hope, acting as if she were indifferent to the situation. Other than disapproving of Sam's relations with her, she might have had only opinion otherwise.

"So, did you do all *this* then…? Ja'hari gestured in a circular motion in Hope's general direction. "Because boy, you know that's against the rules, right? It doesn't work out well for us." Then she crossed her arms over her chest again, seeming to grow even more annoyed with the situation. "I don't know who she is, but she's gots to go." She made a twirling motion in the air, before placing both hands on her hips. She seemed to speak with her hands almost as much as she used words. Sam didn't return to the door, but he did lean backward on a small table beside it.

"Ja that's a'nough. That ain't a discussion and ya ain't me mum." Sam was calm as always, but something in his voice was firm, as if the girl didn't hold as much power as he did in the apartment or life in general. Hope couldn't really be sure which. Ja'Hari looked back and forth between the two of them. She narrowed her eyes, still trying to figure out the situation. She finally settled her gaze on Sam, seeming to quietly study his resolve for a while.

"Explain." She finally said to him, seeming to understand now that this was more than she had originally thought. She had caught on that there was something beyond just her friend making out and marking some girl he barely knew. "I know what you did, I can feel it. I can see." She seemed to be sorting out what pieces she already knew in her mind and trying to sift through what made sense to her. "What would make you risk the wrath a both sides, Amun-Ra *and* Anubis, to give a human 'the sight'?" Hope recognized the names, but to use them in the context in which she did, with a man who once was an angel of the Lord, seemed very odd to her. It made Hope consider what happens when theology merged with mythology, how did such things translate? Ja'Hari spoke of the two as if they were physical entities, not simply abstract gods. So, if the Egyptian gods existed and the God of Heaven, angels, and demons existed, how did it all piece together. Ja'Hari kept looking at Sam with irritation. However,

Sam seemed to be paying attention to both women and saw the confusion in Hope's eyes. Though she also seemed to him to be caught in her own thoughts.

"Mikey and Lucy don' a run a show no more an' I'ma tired a gettin' a left-over bollocks full a shite in a war that I ain't even a part a no more. So ya can stay in a middle an' ride it out, but I ain't bloody doin' it." He seemed perturbed now, enough that he defensively crossed his arms over his chest and glared back at her.

"So, you gunna give the sight to all the humans out there and hope they choose the right side to help?" Ja'Hari began to move around uneasily, almost like a lioness pacing in a cage, mulling over her thoughts. "Sam, you know how unpredictable humans are and even if you could sway them one way or another, they don't have anything invested in this shit. They have their rules, we have ours. That's the way it's always been, and you've seen what happens when they are allowed to see our world. Everyone gets hurt, they freak out, involving them in this has never worked out. That's why He took their sight away in the first place. Getting her involved will only get her killed in the long run."

"She's already in, before I done what I done." Sam said flatly. "Not jus' a witness neither. This's already 'er war, I jus' gave 'er a better weapon." Something he said in that reply caught Ja'Hari off guard.

"She's Talyâ d'Alâhâ?" Her eyes went wide, her face seemed to grow paler all of a sudden. Almost as if in defeat, she crouched down, seeming to try to lower her center of gravity and keep her balance. "Sam..." She paused, staring blankly at the floor. "I truly don't know if you did something really good or *really* bad…" She blinked, fixed on the spot she had been staring at. "It's one thing to give a rando 'the sight'…it's another to give Talyâ d'Alâhâ 'the sight'." Her gaze quickly shot up to Sam. "If they weren't gunning for her before, Amon-Ra and Anubis, will be out for blood. No questions. No hesitation. She'll be dead, we'll be dead for helping her…" Ja'Hari finally looked at Hope, concerned. "Girl, no offense, but I ain't generally the kind of woman that sticks her neck out at risk of personal damage…" She seemed to now study Hope. "Sam wasn't either till now, but…now we're already involved, so it's our heads too that's gunna roll if the sides figure this out." She seemed to suddenly remember some-thing, then tossed a glance toward Sam. "She chosen yet?" To this, Sam shook his head in a 'no' gesture. Ja'Hari put a hand to her forehead, looking back toward where she had focused on earlier. "So, you gave her 'the sight' before you ever even knew what side she was on.?" She blinked a few times; her voice was starting to get nervous.

"I know what side she's on." He stood, walked over to her, and placed his hand gently on her shoulder. "She's on our side. We ain't never had a Talyâ d'Alâhâ on our side. Now we do." He shrugged and moved over to sit beside Hope on the couch once more. "…an it's about time." Ja'Hari shook her head 'no', without looking up.

"I don't know, Sam. We don't have an army. Tum'ah Dām ain't come together since The Garden, we've no guarantee of what'll happen, and we've no guarantee what'll happen when the proverbial shit hits the fan." In that moment, she seemed to make some sort of decision. Standing, she addressed Hope in a way she hadn't before. Ja'Hari's eyes were now much softer, her pupils dilated so that Hope could barely see the green in them, her entire expression had changed. "Fine. Thirty-five hundred years and you still roping me into some kinda bullshit. I got you, though." She straightened up her stature and a determined look crossed her face. "All right, do it. Get all up in my business like you know you want to. No sense in playing a guessing game when you don't have to." Hope knew exactly what she was talking about, no explanation seemed necessary, as the white light welled up inside her, pouring through the fabric of her shirt both in her chest and back, and to the other side, making the symbols impossible to miss. Her eyes also again began to give off a white glow. Something about it seemed to spook Ja'Hari a little, but she kept standing there, allowing Hope to study her. Hope assumed it made her feel vulnerable, in a way, for Hope to have the ability to see beyond the outside to what was underneath.

Still new to all of this, she tilted her head to the side, looking the woman up and down. She blinked a few times, but really wasn't surprised with what she saw. Looking at the woman with 'the sight', she could see underneath, Ja'Hari was completely different than the outer façade appeared. The first thing Hope noticed were the long ears, similar to a fennec fox, though they were the same shade of black as her hair. A long, thin tail of the same color impatiently twitching behind her. Hope's light faded as she finished studying her hidden features. When Hope saw the world through her new power, the reality of each creature, gave off an ethereal appearance that surrounded their human-esque form.

"Satisfied?" Ja'Hari crosses her arms over her chest, trying not to look at Hope, but seemed to be still fighting an internal battle. Though this single word extended an invite into the conversation, that she hadn't made before. When she thought Hope was just an average everyday human, she spoke to and around her as if she were someone else's pet. That single title seemed to transform Hope into an actual person in Ja'Hari's eyes. It somewhat annoyed Hope, but in the current world she now existed in, she couldn't afford to be easily offended. Plus, to an extent, she somewhat understood. She could imagine, to creatures like Sam and Ja'Hari, humans were temporary, powerless, ignorant of the *real* world, and quite possibly a bit of an annoyance.

"I guess." Hope figured she would take what she could get.

"You guess?" The cat-like woman seemed as if the statement offended her. "Girl, I ain't let someone check me for hundreds of years. You'd do well to at least be appreciative." She stopped, narrowing her eyes at Hope, but when she began speaking again, one could tell it was for Sam. "She's green, but...there's something there I can't quite put my finger on..." She seemed concerned, confused, and curious all at once. Sam just nodded in reply. The girl took a deep breath and rolled her eyes, glancing to Hope. "You can call me 'Hari, most do." She said this while moving in the direction she had been going earlier and seeming to decide the argument wasn't worth her time anymore. "Sam, cover your butt, bud. Keep in mind who you are and everybody else too." With that, she disappeared from view. Hope still wasn't sure if 'Hari was approving or disapproving of her. Her eyes moved to Sam, who was staring in the direction 'Hari had gone, but his face was blank, as if he were off in his own world.

"Sam...?" A part of her still felt a rush of adrenaline coursing through her system, a part of her wanted to finish what they had started before the other woman came in. Another part of her knew that probably wasn't going to happen now. Sam was pulled from his thoughts as she spoke to him.

"Hm...?" He looked at her, the same soft, but knowing curiosity in his eyes that he always had when he looked at her. Their eyes connected and a silent warmth passed between them for several moments. He blinked a few times and then offered up a statement. "She's not like that once you get a know 'er..." He seemed to be trying to convince himself of this almost as much as he was trying to convince her.

Little else was said before there came another knock at the door. This knock was hard and almost angry. It sent chills down Hope's spine and caused Sam to jump, before either of them even knew who was behind it.

"Expecting anyone else?" Hope asked, but she didn't need an answer. By the way Sam was staring at the door, as if it might bite him, it was clear he wasn't. There was a nagging pulse in the corner of Hope's eyes, and she could tell that it was her newly gained sight that she wasn't quite in control of yet. She wasn't sure whether others saw the things she did when she saw supernatural type things; or if the supernatural beings simply saw these things all of the time. She did know what the pulsing red meant, and it wasn't something she was sure she was ready to face quite yet. Here it was though, true evil, she was about to face something that the natural order and God had placed into the 'damned' category.

She was nervous and intrigued all at the same time. What she expected and what she received, shockingly, were two completely different sets of circumstances.

Sam slowly opened the door, revealing a young man leaning against the doorframe. He was well dressed in a pressed, pin-striped suit with a matching fedora. He did not wear a tie, instead he had a grey vest over a crisp white shirt giving him a very clean look. Hope hadn't yet seen Sam as outwardly nervous as he seemed to be in this moment.

"Aren't you going to invite me in, Samael?" His voice was pleasant, but arrogant. He didn't wait for Sam to answer, before making a slight gesture of dismissal with his hand. "Scratch that, this isn't a casual type visit." He slammed his hand against the frame he leaned on, which caused the entire room to flash, sending red sparks flying everywhere. After which, the man simply walked in, as if he hadn't just easily broken through all of Sam's wards. When he was fully in the room, he removed his hat, bringing it behind him to hold in the small of his back. The other held onto this wrist. There was an awkward, intentional, silence as the man began to make his way through the room, purposefully looking over everything except the individuals sharing the room with him. Sam seemed shocked that he had broken the seals so easily and just stood there staring at him. When the man finally stopped and once again faced Sam, he rolled his eyes and shook his head. "Oh, come now, Samael, you can't have truly believed that would hold against me…? He offered a breathy half laugh, before looking toward him with amusement over his features.

Hope tried to hold her gifts in check, partly so as not to be rude, but also hoping this being could not figure out who she was. She couldn't gather much about him without the sight, but she felt *something.* He was obviously very powerful, apparently some sort of major player in this war. He was very attractive and young looking, his appearance would suggest that he was no more than nineteen or twenty years of age, though Hope knew better than to trust human sight. He had tousled chocolate brown hair, miraculously having been kept from flattening beneath his hat, which he still held behind him. His feet were spread apart a short distance, his stance holding a graceful, authoritative propriety. Though it wasn't that of a gentleman, more that of a predator. His skin was a porcelain white, perfect and unblemished. His frame was thin but seemed as if he were someone who could do much more damage than most might realize, in a physical altercation. He had high cheekbones and a cleft in his chin. The man didn't glance in her direction, oddly enough though, but she could tell he was very aware of her presence.

"You know, I do not appreciate the deception from you, Samael. I would expect it from The Architect, but not from you." He hung his head enough to show his annoyance and slowly shook it in a disapproving manner. His tone of voice, word usage, and accent was upper class New Englandish in nature.

"I was gunna tell ya. I was jus' tryin' a get more information before I brought 'er to ya..." Sam started to speak but stopped quickly as the man in front of him put a finger to his own lips in a shushing motion, then dropped his hand.

"You weren't." He moved his index finger back and forth in a tisk gesture. "I understand, Samael. You owe me nothing, your allegiance doesn't have to lie with me. You always did look out for number one, right?" Narrowing his eyes on Sam, he allowed another awkward pause between them.

"...'Deus, is not like all that. I was jus'..." Again, Sam was not truly allowed to speak. Hope's curiosity was triggered by recognition of the name. So, this was the infamous Asmodeus, one of the seven Princes of Hell. This meant she most assuredly should keep her gift in check. From what she understood, it was going to be bad enough if the demon realized she was an undecided part of this war, it could likely be so much worse if he realized Sam had given her 'The Sight', as well. Though, at this point, she wasn't sure what he knew. Asmodeus brought his hand up, motioning for Sam to stop, however didn't address him again, instead he turned toward Hope. He took a few steps forward, reaching out his hand, palm side up toward her.

"Asmodeus. Pleasure." His deep brown eyes held a fire behind them, but not the white light Sam's held, instead a crimson glow caused the brown to seem black, but it quickly subsided. Hope allowed him to take her hand, to be polite, but the pit growing in her stomach caused her to not even want to be near the man. He didn't shake, merely held onto it for a moment, before breaking out into a laugh. "You didn't." Asmodeus lifted his hand to his forehead, placing his index finger and his thumb to his temples. His words seemed exasperatedly strained, but his tone remained calm. He looked back toward Sam. "You can't have known, I suppose, but the coincidence of it all is too much." He kept chuckling under his breath, shaking his head, moving toward the window, and stared outside for a few moments. "This changes the rules. Millions of years and who would have thought it would once again be you to unravel 'The Divine Plan'." He turned, bringing his hat in front of him, and once again holding it with both hands. "Seems that old habits never die, do they, Samael?"

Sam stared hard at Asmodeus, seeming confused and determined.

"Changes the rules?" Sam genuinely didn't seem to understand what the demon was talking about and seemed semi-reluctant to speak.

"Yes, yes." 'Deus gave Sam a waving gesture, seeming one of dismissal. "See? This is why things never work out for you all." The man seemed to be at the beginning of a monologue, one that Hope was not sure she really wanted to be privy to. "Good, bad, it's all within the eye of the beholder." He threw his hands to the sides in a slight shrug, then tilted his head to the side. "What is good? What is evil?" He ended with an 'aha' motion, pointing his finger at Hope. "I will tell you what is evil. Evil is a war that goes on since the beginning of time. Evil is knowing the end score and keeping it hidden while you watch the pain and suffering of the world like a reality TV show." He shook his head quickly this time, closing his eyes, and upon opening them again he stared at Hope as if he were looking into her soul. "Evil is forcing your children to tear each other apart by dangling the family fortune in front of them, without telling them the rules of the game or even the objective." He broke his stare on Hope and glanced back toward Sam. "You know it's true. You also know that In

Libro Inferos has been keeping the record since Genesis and further back into what we have been able to piece together before that."

"In Libro Inferos?" Hope could barely get out more than a whisper, but her voice seemed to catch Asmodeus off guard.

"She speaks! Finally decided to join the conversation now, have we? Good, good, the more the merrier. Though you really must pardon my spotty memory, millions of years going through the same endless monotony over and over again, can cause one to forget some tiny details." He made a circular motion. "That truly is the real Hell, you know. Just this never-ending boredom that eats away at your mind..." Suddenly, he made the motion of an explosion with his hands, while continuing to hold onto his hat. "...then you just pop, like a cork." He took a deep breath, nodding his head with what almost seemed sadness, but was short lived. "We all play our part, don't we, Samael?" He raised an eyebrow, questioningly toward Sam, then gracefully slid his hat back on his head. "In any case, I really must be going. Things to do, places to be, people to find." He gave a wink to Hope. "I'll be seeing you later, carissimi unum ." Before he left, he addressed Sam for the last time during this encounter. "You may want to do some reading and soul searching, Samael. You have begun a chain of events that I don't believe you're prepared for. Also..." He motioned toward the walls that had previously held the sigils. "You might want to get that fixed." Asmodeus grinned at Sam, as he made an intentional dig to remind the man of 'his place' in the order of things, after which he walked in the direction of the outside. Sam closed the door behind him, the action of his palm landing on the closed door, made the symbols light back up again as if branding themselves into the walls, before settling back to invisibility. Without another word, Sam plopped down as if he had been defeated.

"Are you alright?" Hope asked him, concerned.

"Yeah, I'm good." He wasn't his emotions were written all over his face.

"What did he mean about changing the game? What happened? Is it because of me?" Hope searched through her thoughts, she knew she wasn't going to be the person to figure this puzzle out, but that didn't stop her from trying to search her mind for possible answers.

"I dunno." Sam frowned. "I should 'a known, but I don't." He seemed angry with himself. "I seen a book from a dis'ance, but few get'a read it. We gunna have ta find out before 'Deus gets his."

"Who would know about something like that? Something that is above your pay grade? There can't be many, right?" She had to follow his lead, because she didn't even have an inkling as to what they should do next.

"Ya'd be surprised, Deifilia. I think I got someone could tell me what it said." The man seemed distracted. "Won't be a fun trip an' I gotta make a stop first. I need ya keys."

Sam's driving was just how she had imagined it would be, distracted and determined. It wasn't long before he pulled the car into a parking spot. Hope looked out of the window and then got out when he turned the car off, somewhat confused as to why they were here. She stared at the large hospital in front of them and watched as Sam made his way toward it.

She caught up to him quickly, even though Sam's gait was much faster than her own.

"There's someone here that can help? Do you know someone who works here or are you visiting a patient?" Again, Hope threw questions at him much more quickly than he could answer. In response, Sam stopped and looked at her, seeming frustrated, because she was distracting him from his purpose.

"Ya 'ave ta let me answer one question 'fore ya ask anotha, 'ope." The girl's face went somber. It was the first time he'd ever used her actual name. He'd always used his own nicknames for her, which let her know that this situation was serious, and she needed to adjust to his level of alertness. "In a way, someone can 'elp." He left it at that, without answering the last few questions. Hope decided to keep quiet and just follow for now. Sam led her to an elevator and pushed a button to take them to the third floor. As they were waiting, Hope's curiosity grew and she wanted so badly to ask him more questions, but he'd made himself clear that he was not in the mood. So, she decided to keep them to herself for now.

The two exited the elevator quickly. Sam began walking much slower, glancing inside the rooms as he went. After more than a few rooms had been passed by, he motioned for her to stay out in the hallway. Several minutes passed by before anything happened, but then a bright flash of white light caught her attention, and medical alarms within the room notified the area that something was wrong. A figure came quickly from the room, grabbed Hope's arm, and swept her into the elevator. When the doors closed behind them, the girl finally had the opportunity to look back at Sam, except it wasn't Sam.

"What in the Hell?! Where is Sam?!" She was startled to see a completely different face looking back at her. The man was wearing Sam's clothes, but they were loose on him. The stranger tapped at his temple, motioning toward his eye. Hope's eyes lit up and for a moment she envisioned the gift as something of a garage door opener. The sight revealing the man's true form, the situation slowly fading into view, something that couldn't have been seen unless she had opened that door. Though what she saw, when the sight flooded into view startled her. "Sam?!" Other than the glow he gave off and his broken angelic features, she couldn't really *see* anything different than she had without the sight. It was more the feeling she had when she flipped that switch. The feeling of familiarity, comfort, connection...the feeling of connecting with the soul beyond the human casing.

"Yeah, we gotta bounce in a hurry." He almost pulled her along when the elevator opened, rushing to the door. "Once they find Evan, they're going to lock this place down."

Hope was speechless, she hadn't thought that anything could surprise her anymore, but she wasn't even sure how she was expected to react to this situation. He ushered her into the car and started it without a single wasted moment. Once they were on the road and a few blocks away, the man's demeanor relaxed.

"Who's Evan?" The girl asked quietly, now that the danger had passed, and it was just the two of them again. Sam let out a single breath of a laugh.

"All the questions that I'm sure you have at the moment and your question to me is, who's Evan? Do you mean that in an abstract sense, a literal sense, or the personal sense?" Sam's answer was rhetorical. She furrowed her brows and looked at him, letting him know that his jokes were not appreciated at the moment. He lifted his fingers off of the steering wheel long enough to make a 'have it your way' gesture. "Evan was a donor."

"A donor? What do you mean, a donor? A whole-body donor?" She seemed to still have some mental wires that weren't connecting, possibly because she'd had so many supernatural experiences lately, she wasn't sure she could even try to process any more. She was confused and a bit annoyed.

"Yeah. Sort of." Sam seemed somewhat ashamed for a moment, knowing he should have at least warned her about what he'd intended on doing. It had been selfish not to tell her, but she might have tried to stop him, and he didn't have the luxury of considering her feelings at the moment.

"How can you just take someone else's body...like it belongs to you or something?! What gives you the right to do that? What if he wasn't finished with it? Did he say it was okay or did you even ask him?" Hope wasn't sure how it worked, but all she could think about was the 'Edgar Suit' the 'bug' wore in the movie Men in Black. Sam shook his head, the frustration in his eyes growing. He wasn't upset with her. He was upset with himself.

"It's not like that. It's a vessel." Sam's answers stayed short and sweet, seeming to be figuring out how to explain it to her.

"A vessel? You mean like it wasn't a person, that body

was just there for you to use?" It wasn't the craziest possible scenario, she knew it wasn't the truth, but she needed something logical right now. Her *rational* thinking told her that she was in the car with a murder right now, though she knew that wasn't really true either.

"It was. He was gone. Alex left this world months ago, his body was alive because of the machines, but his soul was long gone." Sam glanced to Hope to make sure she was alright. "It's the easiest way now. It used to be harder, and we had to be less selective...and quick. A few seconds between departure and death, now there are whole wards of vessels" He took a deep breath. "They don't wake up, you know. They never wake up. When someone wakes up from a coma, it's never been the original soul returning. We have their brain, their memories...enough to blend into their lives, but they don't come back." He stared at the road, even though he could feel her eyes on him. "It's like buying an old computer and putting a new operating system in. All your files are there, but the system that it uses isn't the same anymore."

"Okay." She spoke only a single word, but she meant it. It wasn't sarcastic or saying something that she knew he wanted to hear, the word dripped with acceptance.

"Okay?" He asked, confused at her lack of continuance.

"Okay." She blinked a few times, as she recognized where they were going. She wasn't sure she was ready to deal with Leonardo again so soon, but she supposed she would have to be ready eventually. She might as well get it over with and rip it off like a Band-Aid.

7

Once they pulled up to the house, Sam almost jumped out of the vehicle and didn't wait on Hope to head for the door. He pounded on it loudly, trying to get immediate attention. Once Hope reached the door, she opened it and walked inside, leaving the door open for Sam.

"Come on." She spoke to him, looking behind her at the angel just standing there beyond the doorway.

"Can't." Sam replied.

"Why not?" Hope asked.

"Have to be invited." Again, Sam's answer was quick.

"Oh, well come in then." To this, the angel slowly shook his head. "Why can't you come in if I invite you?"

"...because it is not *your* home, not *your* wards." A voice came from behind Hope, inside the house. "Right, Samael?" Leonardo had apparently pegged him as the fallen as soon as he had seen him. Sam simply rolled his eyes. Hope figured it like was likely Leo had seen him play musical bodies before and knew tells that Hope hadn't caught yet. Leo crossed his arms over his chest. "Come in. What do you want?" As always, the man seemed frustrated at having to pause his day for others.

"I need to make a call." Sam walked on inside. Leonardo didn't even seem to react to Sam's change of body or, at least, not outwardly so.

"You have a cell phone. There are pay phones. Go make a call somewhere else." Leo's tone suggested that he knew what Sam meant but wasn't wanting to acknowledge what the angel was talking about.

"Dude, I don't have time for this. You know what I mean, we all know you built it. Your arrogance convinced you that we didn't know about it, but we all know." Sam paused for a brief second, throwing his arms out in frustration with the man in front of him. "Besides, you're not there yet, but you're on the right track. Once you finish it, you might have some issues with safeguarding it, but until then you're sitting on a huge golden cell phone that can make a toll-free call to the clouds or the pit...maybe even a few places in between."

"Jeez, you're both giving me a headache." Hope had considered a long walk off of a short cliff several times in the last couple of days and this moment was far from an exception. They both stopped to look at Hope who had her thumb and middle fingers, of her left hand placed tightly on her temples. Leo finally seemed to give in.

Once they were down in the room with the beautiful machine, Sam went directly to the controls, dialing in some very specific coordinates. As a reaction, the glistening rings began to spin faster and faster, twisting amongst themselves, until they moved so quickly that one could only see a golden glow, as the rings disappeared within its speed.

"Ytzr kshr, Gabriel." Sam spoke loudly and directly into the golden orb. "Might want to close your eyes." Leo's eyes were already closed and Hope quickly closed her own, heeding his warning without question. She didn't know what he was doing, but she figured this was one of those times she should trust the angel and that the 'Architect' knew what he was talking about.

Hope could see a flash of light so bright that it seemed like daylight under her closed eyelids. When the light slowly dimmed, Hope opened her eyes to see the machine had abruptly stopped and there now was a fourth person in the room.

Gabriel didn't make any attempt to hide any of himself, a set of six wings behind him in proud, full view. They were truly beautiful and more alluring than anything she'd ever seen. Before she even realized it, her newly gifted internal light seemed to react to the creature and began to glow from deep within her. It almost felt like a supernatural boner, she had absolutely no control over it. Gabriel didn't acknowledge her yet, instead he directed his full attention on Samael.

"Brother." The angel began, in what almost seemed a disappointed tone. The expression he wore over his features, though muted, was as if he were looking over the black sheep of his family. The man was tall, much taller than Leo or Sam. His strawberry, blonde hair fell in short ringlets around his face. He was shirtless, but wore very simple, white pants. Hope couldn't imagine there would be a shirt in the world that would allow for his large corporal wings. Unlike Sam's broken stubs, Gabriel's wings were solid and looked so soft that it took conscious will power on her part not to reach out and touch them. Unlike the many religious paintings, the girl had seen, the halo of this creature was not simply around his head. The blue light lit up the entire space around his body and pulsed with raw power, so much so that it gave her goosebumps instinctively. She was speechless, with a combination of emotions, her stomach flip flopping inside of her. Her thoughts at war with each other. He inspired awe, but he also caused a feeling of fear and nervousness, a feeling of security and danger all at once. "Why have you called me to this place? Do you not understand we fight a war in that the home of your creation?"

"I understand, but we need you here...now." Sam motioned to the humans in the room. Gabriel seemed to minimally acknowledge the others. Leo seemed unphased by the appearance of the Archangel, as he seemed with most things. Hope could not stop staring, wide eyed. The angel's eyes caught hers and for several moments, they stared at each other. His pure white irises felt as if they were looking deep into her soul.

"It has begun." He pulled his gaze from Hope and moved it to Sam again. "He knew it would be you. Always it is you, Samael." Gabriel took a deep, somewhat unnecessary breath, sighing as he let it out.

"Father?" He paused, only receiving a shake of golden curls in response. "What has begun?" Sam didn't seem to understand. Hope could tell by his reaction that he wasn't privy to near as much information as his brother.

"Michael." Gabriel spoke a single name, which caused Sam to furrow his brows and look downward. "Uriel considered it would be Andras, he has after all, fallen much further than you. His would have been for reasons much different than your own." A small twitch began in Sam, avoiding his brother's sight. "Michael knew it would be you to open the gateway, though quite a bit ahead of our assumed schedule." Gabriel narrowed his eyes on him. "And so, it is written that one of the fallen shall bring a touched mortal into the light…" Gabriel lifted a hand to his brother's cheek, raising Sam's line of vision, allowing him to see the expression on his brother's face. "It has always been written in the books you were not allowed to read. It also means I must sound the horn, for the time foretold is neigh." Sam blinked as if in shock, unsteady on his feet for a moment. "It is not to be feared, brother, for you have chosen the will of our Father. It is for this reason; you are to be rewarded." Sam's eyes lit up. "Slow, Samael. The reward you seek is far too great for this battle won, but you have chosen your champion and your cause well." Gabriel moved his hand from the side of Sam's face and to his forehead, again sparking the blinding light, catching Hope off guard. When her eyes finally started fading back into spotty, sparkled vision, something about Sam had changed. He was in the same body he had taken from the hospital, but Gabriel had restored his wings to him, and his light seemed a bit brighter than it had been. The wings were in ethereal sight only, without solid form, and his light remained white. His eyes for a mere moment matched the other angel's, but then slowly faded back to the way they had been. "For now, you must hide these gifts restored to you, but you will need them for the time that is to come." He then left his brother and moved to Leo. "Leonardo. Your machine has proved invaluable, and so shall it be made into what it was intended, with also the protection of Heaven's Army. You have been gifted with much wisdom but have lacked the spark of life for your long-suffered struggle. We are in debt to your service and would gift you with that of which you seek." Gabriel reached his hand to the man, as a response Da Vinci examined it, before taking it. Leo's yellow glow flashed bright, though not as much as the gift he'd given Sam. His entire body seemed to crackle and spark. "You should have no need for these potions any longer, but the promise of eternal youth does not promise eternal life. Your time will no longer be prolonged on our accord, it is now up to you how long you choose to fight." Finally, it was Hope's turn, and she could feel herself blushing. Every ounce of her quivered with anxiousness as he made his way to her. "Talyâ d'Alâhâ." He paused, watched her, and then made an action that none of them could have predicted. Gabriel swiftly took her in his arms and embraced her, one arm around her torso, the other holding the back of her head in his hand. She stiffened, now able to feel the pillowy softness of the six, folded wings behind him. He whispered something to her that the other two could not hear, then loosened his grip some and his own blue glow began to pour through her, spilling from the symbols on her chest and from her eyes. "Take care of them...and choose your warriors wisely, for you now have the knowledge of Heaven, Hell, and the Earth behind you. Guard it well and trust yourself above all others." With those last few words, Gabriel stepped back and in another bright flash, he was gone.

The three, once they were again able to see, after the blindingly bright light without warning, remained silent for a while. They considered what had just transpired, each in their own individual way.

"I know what we have to do." Hope was the first to break the silence, whereas Sam seemed distracted with reveling in his semi-returned angel accessories and Leo seemed in his head about something. "*I know what we have to do!*" She yelled to get their attention. The raised voice resulted in the expected outcome, both men looked at her with a mixture of annoyance, confusion, and inquiry. "We have to go to Hell."

Sam placed his hands on his face, in an exasperated motion.

"How do you expect us to do that?" He asked, speaking beneath his hand. "We came here to avoid Asmodeus and now you want to just march right in there?" Leo rolled his eyes at the possibility of interjected humor, as Sam saluted him.

"March?" Hope narrowed her eyes; she had assumed that getting into Hell would be a bit more complicated than just walking through the gates.

"I like marching much better than Waltzing…" He paused for a moment, then added. "…and I'm not feminine enough to Sashay. So yes, march." He nodded in a matter-of-fact way. Hope shook her head, trying not to crack a smile. Without warning, Sam slid in her direction and began singing, while beginning to stiffly march, yet somehow it seemed almost a dance.

"Mine eyes have seen the glory of the coming of the hoard, we're gunna trample out the fences where Earth's fate of wrath is stored! We're stocking up on whiskey 'cause we're gunna meet our Lord! His truth--" Leo interrupted Sam's boisterous rendition of Battle Hymn of the Republic, seeming to be unable to handle any more of the angel's nonsense in a time he considered serious.

"That's about enough, we need a plan, we need to know what tools we can combine to increase our odds of getting in and out of the gate alive." Leo moved to the desk within the Centrenarithan room, shuffling through some papers that were there.

"Oh, come the Hell on, Italian Stallion, loosen up, we have back up, it's a win." With Leonardo distracted again, Samael began to sing and march-dance as if he'd been there and celebrated when the song originated. "GLORY, GLORY HALLELUJAH! GLORY, GLORY HALLELUJAH!" He pointed to her as he sang loudly, as if dedicating his performance to her while also trying his best to annoy Leo, he faded off at the end into humming the song and less exaggeratedly danced to himself. "His troops are marching on." He seemed pumped, a high contrast to the beaten down creature that had been in the same room with Asmodeus a very short while ago. She supposed he had more than enough reason to feel better about his existence, but the angel was certainly unpredictable and odd. To an extent, she liked that about him. Da Vinci was predictable, calculated, and sometimes boring. Hope couldn't predict many of her 'guardian angel's' actions or motives. She used the term guardian angel loosely. At the same time, just as Leo said, she did trust him...but she didn't intend on trusting him with everything.

"So let me get this straight, your plan begins with snagging the key to the gate from Asmodeus?" Sam sat in an older leather office chair, within Leo's library. Hope sat in one almost identical to it, to his left. Leo was behind his desk, his fingers pressed together forming something like a triangle in front of his face, his elbows resting on top of papers strewn about the desktop. "Tell me, Leo, what about that doesn't seem crazy to you. That sounds absolutely insane, to me. Are you feeling okay, man?" The angel stood up and reached toward Leonardo's pursed forehead as if he were going to check for a fever. In response, the man swatted him away.

"Do you happen to have a better idea?" The question was obviously rhetorical. Samael acted as if he was about to say something, but Leo didn't wait for an answer. "We need to consider all of the variables in the situation." He stood, beginning to pace and speak with his hands, almost as if he were translating his thoughts into something the other two could understand. "The elements in our favor are…" He moved to a chalkboard and semi-feverishly began something that seemed to be a list. He wrote in cursive English, but in his haste, it was messier than his normal handwriting. "Myself, or The Architect, as I am referred to by most involved parties. Samael, or as I am herewith going to refer to him as 'The Redeemed Fallen' which also plays a prospective part in the plan…" He stopped himself from going in the direction of a tangent and made swirling motion with his hand. "…but that is something that can be extrapolated upon at a later time." He paused long enough to write it upon the board. "And Hope…" Da Vinci turned, and a piercing gaze was directed toward her, seeming to search through his mind for any other option beyond his original plan, considering he hadn't vocalized every detail to the other two within the room yet, he had time to change his mind. He gave his head a quick shake, knowing that the probability of success for any other option was dramatically lower than his original plan. "Hope is an undecided . She can get closer to Asmodeus than either of us can, at this time."

"Absolutely not, there's no way I'm letting her go in there alone. She's not ready for that kind of fight yet. If he found out the reason she was there, the amount of Hell he'd rain on her would be astronomical. Death would be more merciful, because he probably wouldn't show her any." Sam sat up in his chair and protested against it heatedly.

"I do not like it either, Sam." Leo's words were almost a growl in response. There was a protective tone in the words of both males that went beyond just the defense of a friend. It was something that was realized by both in that moment, they both became silently frustrated in their own way, then dropped the argument, for now. Da Vinci's next words were very matter of fact. "If there were any other way, do you not think that I would have considered it? Asmodeus is already suspicious of me, he has been for many years now. He knows our arrangement is just business, give and take. He will sense that I am not in need of his 'services' any longer and then all trust will be obsolete." Leonardo sat back down in his chair, still seeming perturbed, but also compartmentalizing his frustrations for a time when it might be more appropriate. "He knows you have no true allegiance to him, he may have wanted it and tried to pry it from you, but he knows you could break that leash if you wanted to. He was only able to keep you on that chain, because aside from his offer, you had no other options. Low level angels, demons, and the unaligned you might be able to keep the secret Gabriel, but to a Knight, you're going to reek of holy blessing. I am human and I can sense the difference in you. Granted, this is mainly because I have known you for quite a time, but if you thought he would not notice, you would likely be incorrect. Beside the fact, would it really be worth risking failure before we even get close to keep the girl out of the way of harm? She is already in this! Half of both sides already want her dead, we both know it and until she has 'chosen a side' to reassure those who think there are no grey areas, she is our best weapon..." He paused for one more moment, before adding what he considered a final blow. "Plus, though she may not know how to use them yet, with the endowment you gave her and the contribution of Gabriel, the girl is probably the most *powerful* weapon we have at this point." This statement made Leo's brow furrow. He didn't seem to like any of that statement. It was almost like it left a terrible taste in his mouth as he spoke it.

"Why don't we let *her* decide?" Hope finally decided to join in the conversation. "Leo's right, not necessarily about the power thing, but as far as Asmodeus is concerned, he doesn't seem afraid of me. He spoke to me at Sam's house almost as if he were trying to charm me to his side and we can use that." When she mentioned being at Samael's house, she could see a twinge of jealousy fall over The Architect's face, but she couldn't focus on that now. "Just tell me what I need to do."

The night was dark, without a moon or stars, brisk with a great deal of moisture that hung in the air. It was the kind of night that just made a person want to curl up in front of a fire with a good book. This night in particular though, was different, tonight could be her saving grace or it could be a grave mistake. Hope opened the car door with a creaking sound. She had parked the blue Firebird in front of the empty lot. With the gifts she'd been given, she could now see the masked building in front of her. It was lit up by a faint red glow, assumingly because of the spell-work that hid it from view of the world. The building itself looked old, as if it had been built over a hundred years ago, which seemed to suit, considering what Asmodeus's choice of attire had been when she'd first met him. It was several stories tall and looked almost like an office building, it made her wonder if all sides of this war had buildings such as this hidden from the view of each other. When she tried to open the door, she couldn't. It seemed sealed from the inside, but after barely a second, a voice came from an intercom beside the double doors. She hadn't noticed it before, which made her wonder if it had actually been there before she pulled on the handle or had come about as she did so.

"May I help you?" The voice on the other end was female, obviously not Asmodeus, but she knew she'd likely have to make her way through a gauntlet of underlings before she would get to the 'big boss'. It almost seemed like the plotline to a video game and a part of her was pulsing with adrenaline at the excitement of it all. The anticipation was overwhelming. The anticipation of *what* exactly, she wasn't sure of at this point. She didn't know whether it would go well or badly. She was only sure that she was standing here attempting it, which was exhilarating in and of itself.

"I need to speak with, Asmodeus." Hope responded, not seeing a button near the speaker to push, so she assumed that the woman would hear her just by speaking plainly.

"Do you have an appointment?" The voice on the other end questioned, her tone said it was a very mundane inquiry for the woman.

"No, but I promise you that he will want to speak to me." Hope sighed. For a moment, she considered that this must be what prescription drug reps felt like when they went to big medical groups. She wondered if Asmodeus was the only demon of rank in this building or if this was like a central headquarters or something.

"Asmodeus is not taking visit--" The woman was interrupted and when she came back onto the speaker, her tone had changed. "Asmodeus will see you."

Hope wasn't sure what had happened and why the woman's mind had changed, but as soon as hope heard the click of the door being let loose, she pulled on it again. The inside of the building was similar to what she had imagined it would look like, except for on the walls were the glowing white and blue symbols, similar to what had been on the walls of Sam's apartment and Leo's house, except lacking the red and yellow, which she had ascertained kept evil entities out. As for the yellow symbols, she assumed there was no need due to the fact that, Leo aside, normal humans wouldn't even be aware that the building was even here, much like she wasn't in her first visit. As Hope walked into the main entryway, the woman behind the desk stood, almost as if the girl were royalty, and shuffled her way toward Hope. The attendant looked as if she were a secretary that had fallen right out of the 1920's. She wore a light blue pencil skirt that fell just above the knee and an all-business suit jacket to match. Her hair was blonde and cut with a stylish wave, her skin was a creamy pale, but her aura was a very similar bright red to match the man Hope assumed was her boss.

"Beg pardon, Miss. We weren't expecting you so soon." The woman took Hope to an elevator that seemed very old, with a pull gate and a lever that caused the motor to carry the elevator up and down, similar to Leo's. This seemed odd to Hope, considering what this building held, she had assumed they would be going down.

"It's alright." Hope answered her, trying to seem as un-affected and nonchalant as possible. The girl was trying to portray a confidence that she didn't truly possess, but she thought she was doing quite well at acting as if she did.

The elevator stopped at a mid-level floor and the woman opened the gate without stepping out into the room, motion-ing for Hope to exit. Hope noticed that the woman almost seemed nervous herself, as if she wasn't invited to this party and was scared at the reaction her boss might have to her. Hope walked through the door into a large open room that seemed to encompass the entire level.

"Come in, carissimi unum." Asmodeus's voice echoed through the quiet room, his tone was just as arrogant as it was before, but friendly. "I assumed it would take you longer to drop by, but I can't say that I'm disappointed." He turned his chair around to face her and looked her over in an amused, downcast gaze. The lighting in the room was warm and, even though his aura was as evil as it had been before, the hand-some appearance of the creature couldn't be ignored. She was almost overwhelmed by it, and it gave her skin a warm tingling feeling. It also caused the symbols under her jacket to light up. She wasn't sure whether he had induced it, or it had just been a reaction to being alone with him. Asmodeus stood and moved slowly around to the front of his desk, leaning on it, and crossing one ankle over the other casually. His attire was much different than it had been before, much more contemporary and if she hadn't had the sight, she wouldn't have known he was anything more than what he appeared to be. He wore jeans and a band t-shirt, one of her favorite bands, in fact. She wondered if he truly liked them or if he just knew that she did. There were more than a few moments of silence as they seemed to inspect each other.

Hope had worn an outfit that she intended to distract him with, drawing away from her true purpose. When he seemed to be suspicious, she began to doubt whether she should have walked into the lion's den or not. She had worn a red dress, not tight enough to be uncomfortable, but fitted around the waist, with a belled skirt that fell just past her knees. Red wedge sandals, gleamed in the light and cupped her feet perfectly. Around her shoulders she wore a jacket with three-quarter sleeves, having hoped to hide the symbols, but at this point she had been exposed. Her long purple hair framed her body in gentle waves, giving her a somewhat exotic appearance. That was something that, in fact, seemed to be intriguing to the male demon in front of her.

"You know, you are a curious one." He stood and slowly made his way toward her, in a way which someone might approach a deer. "Not simply Puer Deus, which is a delicious coincidence in and of itself, but so powerful now..." Hope stood still, starting to regret her part in this plan. Leo and Sam couldn't get to her, she was on her own, but she had known she would be from the start. She was beginning to feel outmatched and nervous that she might not be able to follow through. Asmodeus reached to her, sliding the jacket off of her, his hands lightly grazing the symbols around her collarbone as they moved across her shoulders and down her arms. The jacket fell limply to the floor and Hope remained completely still.

The touch of the demon forced so many emotions to course through her, almost like Gabriel's touch, but somehow just the opposite. When Asmodeus touched her, she felt a warmth that rippled through her, igniting every nerve in her body with a desire unlike she'd ever felt before. When the jacket was gone, he again ran his fingers carefully over the symbols. Then in a single quick slide his hands moved around her shoulders and to the symbols on her back, placing his palms firmly to each of them, and pulling her into an embrace. In an instant, power coursed through her, much like when Gabriel had held her, but different. It was almost as if she were feeling the energy of both entities at war within her. It wasn't painful, but it wasn't comfortable either. When his energy retracted and he loosened his grip on her, she couldn't move. It felt as if she had just had the best 'union' of her entire life, but a part of her felt guilty about it and dirty for somewhat enjoying it.

"I am far from stupid, and this war will happen with or without my blessing." He released her; a part of Hope hadn't really wanted him to. "See, Gabe and Sam already have a hand in this, this is me throwing my hat in the ring."

"W-what do you mean?" Hope was still feeling the leftover pulses of the radiant energy he had forced upon her. "What did you do?"

"Nothing that hadn't already been done to you before." He paused, leaned back onto the desk again, then lifted his hand up as if he were inspecting his manicure. "I gave you a gift." He offered her a malicious, furrowed smirk. "You get what you want, I get what I want, everyone goes home happy." He lifted a finger, as if he had just remembered something. Asmodeus reached toward a small box that sat amongst the very organized items on his desk, then tossed it to Hope. She caught it and opened it to see an old looking skeleton key, then looked back at Asmodeus. "That's what you were after, right?" He shrugged. "You shouldn't need it any longer, considering you are now connected to me, but if for any reason I'm not available to you...you have a key to the gates."

"What do you want in return?" Hope wasn't sure what to say or how to react. She had come into the building expecting to seduce the demon and get away with the key to the gate on the sly. She never expected him to simply give it to her. Asmodeus lifted his hand and motioned with his index finger to come toward him. Without even the thought of walking forward, Hope's body moved toward him, until her palms rested on either side of where he leaned against the desk. Bent forward, she was so close to him that she could feel his breath on her lips. He placed his hands on her hips, gliding them slowly over the sides of her body and neck, until they cupped her face.

"Real estate." He whispered before he kissed her. The kiss was long and deep, but not that of a lover, it was more lustful than that and she felt the same sensation as when he had first touched her. She couldn't resist it, for now, he was controlling her movements. It wasn't the same as when he had pushed his influence inside of her, but it gave a faint resemblance. When he let her go, he dropped the control he had over her body, as it seemed the kiss was more a show of the power, he had over her than anything. "You see, the incorporeal world works based on real estate exchange rates. I give you something, you give me something. Gabe and Sam gave you something, but they took something too." He casually spoke with his hands, as she backed away from him a few feet. "What they received was a bit less valuable than it could have been, they couldn't stake a full claim on you without your permission, but a piece of your soul belongs to them. Likewise, I now have a claim on you."

"Like you own a part of me?" Hope was confused and beginning to get upset.

"Not really, it's more like a 'blood brothers' sort of thing. I'm tied to you, you're tied to me, one big happy family. Though, now you're tapped out. Gabe's worked, because your original spiritual brand came from one of the unaffiliated. Now, with my own connection, you are now truly neutral." Deus shrugged. "That's what you wanted, right? True neutral? You didn't want to choose a side, now you don't have to. Normally this is not how we do things, official rules and such, but I figured as long as we're all breaking the rules, I might as well play a part in it."

"So, what do you get out of having a piece of my soul?" Hope still was unsure what the benefit to him was, she knew there had to be more to it than just the ability to be a puppeteer, especially considering, it looked as if it drained him quite a bit to do so.

"There are some side perks, but none worth mentioning for now. I'm sure Samael and Leonardo can fill you in on the details." He took a deep breath. "For now, though, I need to insist on your departure, all of this has taken more out of me than I assumed it would."

For a moment, Hope considered the fact that in this weakened state, it would likely be much easier to kill the demon in front of her, but she wasn't sure what exactly that meant for her current state. If he had laid claim to a piece of her soul, what would that mean if something happened to her or to him? She finally made the decision to simply take her leave. She had gotten what she came for, even if it had happened in a way she hadn't expected. The plan had still been a success, but the repercussions that it might have in the future concerned her.

"Give my regards to Leo and Sam, doll. I'm sure we will all get together again soon..." Asmodeus grinned as she stepped back into the elevator. "...sooner than any of you might expect."

Hope wasn't sure what he meant by that last comment, but as she travelled downward in the elevator to the first floor, she noticed slight differences in things. She hadn't figured out Sam or Gabriel's gifts yet, let alone adding another to it. The biggest difference she noticed when she was able to open the front door. The same door that hadn't budged when she had come in, now opened with ease. Making her way out to the Firebird, she shuffled through so many thoughts that it almost overwhelmed her. She needed a beer, a burger, and a bed. She was definitely on supernatural overload.

8

"He did what?!?" Leonardo's voice echoed through the house, bouncing off of the walls around them, as if it were over a loudspeaker. Hope hadn't even told him about the kiss Asmodeus had forced her into. At the very moment, she kind of felt like a supernatural tramp. Even if the third hadn't been her fault, she couldn't honestly say that she hated it. All of these things caused her mind to wander and even though Leo continued to rant, she wasn't really listening.

She hadn't been back long. She had no idea where Sam had gone, she was still getting used to the 'gifts' she'd been given, but she didn't feel him here. It was probably a good thing. Without her here to mediate, especially with every-thing that had just happened, the two men might have killed each other. The sound of Leo sighing broke Hope from her daze. Mentally he seemed to be moving away from the semi-emotional, protective outburst, as he began to rationalize through the situation.

"I suppose not making an automatic enemy of Asmodeus is a good thing, though without being sure of the exact capa-bilities of each energy that you have absorbed, we are flying blind." Leo crossed the room, pushing on a panel. A latch clicked, releasing the pressure plate, and it caused a hidden drawer to slightly protrude. The 'drawer', if it could even be called that, was as shallow as a surgical tray and, though she couldn't see inside of it, she assumed that it didn't hold office supplies. As he picked up the thin case that had been inside the drawer, he walked toward her with it and placed it on the desk. Now that she could finally see what was there, it was very anticlimactic. Nothing. Nothing was on the tray. Though it did steam slightly, as if it were hot, for some reason she had a strong desire to touch it, but she didn't. Instead, she narrowed her eyes, moving them back and forth between Leo and the tray.

"What are you going to do?" She asked him, with a slight bit of concern in her voice.

"Genetic testing." Leonardo replied nonchalantly, as if it were a mundane activity.

"You can do genetic testing here?" Hope asked confused, even hospitals outsourced their testing, she couldn't under-stand how he was going to do genetic testing right here in the library of his home. Leo spun around on his heels, thrusting his hands out to his sides with a bit of sarcasm.

"Who do you think began that science?" He let out a breath of a laugh. "Paintings." He huffed. "Thousands of sci-entific achievements and you all remember the paintings." He shook his head gathering what seemed like tools to perform the tests he had been speaking of. "I said, Gregor, the human body is made up of cells, but what are those cells made of?" Of course, he would not have remembered it if I hadn't invited him to work the science of the thing with me. The man was a drunkard, a fifth of Russian vodka per night was considered a normal Tuesday." Leo put down the tools he had gathered on the metal plate, which had ceased steaming. "You would be surprised at what I keep to myself these days. I have had a lot of free time over my years." The tools he had brought out looked odd, but she assumed that they would help him figure things out. If she had to endure a little poking and prodding, so be it.

"Ouch!" She jumped as he strapped what seemed like a blood pressure cuff around her arm and she felt a tiny pin prick, as a clear tube began to drain blood from her arm, into a small vile. He filled up five small tubes, while the cuff released and constricted on her arm. When he was finished with the fifth vial, he pressed a button on the cuff and there was a second pin prick. This one she had been somewhat ready for, so she remained silent. Leo removed the cuff, leaving no signs that it had even pierced the skin. It still stung a bit, but other than the sensation it had left behind, there was nothing, not even a red spot.

"The next one is a bit more difficult, but also the most important, in our situation." Leo picked up what looked like a small machine off of the tray, this machine had a vial attached to it and an enormous needle. She hadn't ever seen anything like it before and she doubted there were many, if any, like it elsewhere. "This is not going to feel great." Without another warning, Leo grabbed her left shoulder and thrust the needle hard and directly into the center her chest. It took Hope's breath away and in an instant, she felt something like depression, heartache, and sadness. She felt several overwhelmingly negative feelings all at once. A feeling that she wouldn't have been able to describe well enough to give it true justice. It didn't last long, and Leo yanked the needle back out. When she was able to gather her thoughts again, she looked at the man, mouth agape in something similar to shock. When she was able to focus on him, she saw what he had been after. Inside of the vial was a glowing brightness, a light similar to what she had seen in the mirror. However, now it was a bit different. It seemed to be at war somehow. A swirling mix of energies, like oil and water. It almost looked like a liquid, but then again it didn't. She wasn't sure what it was exactly, but it had come from inside of her. She assumed it was a sample of whatever the three supernatural beings had given her.

"What is that? Is that my soul?" Hope's eyes went wide. Da Vinci rolled his eyes.

"No. It is a grilled cheese sandwich." He shook his head, pulling the glowing vial from the machine and placing it on the tray with the vials of blood. "It is a sample of your soul, like the blood I took." The machine and the cuff he'd used he put to the side of the desk and picked up the tray. Taking a deep breath, he motioned in the direction he started walking. "Come on. I will explain while I work." She followed him as instructed, not necessarily because he told her to do so, but because she was also curious. They moved out of the library and toward one of the few locked doors. "The key is in my pocket." Hope felt awkward about doing so but slid her hand in his pocket to get the key, unlocked the door, and opened it for him. Behind the door was a small metal room, with a set of double doors ahead of them, to their side, a keypad and a palm sized button. "Very carefully, put this code in. It is very specific and dangerous to hit a wrong number, there are no do-overs." Leo still held onto the tray, watching Hope as she moved to the keyboard.

"Ready." Each number that Da Vinci spoke, she repeated before she pressed the number. "Six, eight, six. Seven, eight, four, three. Enter." She hit the buttons as he told her to, which brought up another code box. He instructed her to keep going. "Six, six, si--" She tossed a glare at Da Vinci, before she depressed the button. "Six." There it was, she was wondering when the sign of the beast would show up, how clever of him to include it in his passcode. She hit the enter key, whereas there was no space for another digit, then continued to the third set of numbers. "Eight, seven, two, six, seven, four, three, eight." Immediately after she hit the enter button for a last time and a burst of air came from the ceiling. It was forceful and smelled like a tattoo shop. More likely it was the smell of green soap to sterilize themselves and any-thing they might be bringing inside of the testing room. She knew it because it was one of her favorite smells in the whole world. There was nothing like the smell of a clean tattoo shop and it was something that one could never forget. When the air jets finished, the doors slid open with a mechanical whine, as if they needed some WD40. The room inside was pure white and very large. She was almost afraid to walk on the white floor, for fear of possibly getting it dirty.

"It was a good thing that you put in the codes correctly. Otherwise, we would have had a shower of corrosive acid instead." He said as if it were normal and not a big deal.

"Good to know." Hope blinked stopping in her tracks, unsure if he was being serious or not. Though, the man didn't truly seem like the joking kind, at least not within the few days she had known him.

Once they were both inside, Da Vinci didn't waste any time getting to his lab table and the machines thereon. Hope, on the other hand, fell back and examined things in the room. It looked like a miniature hospital. She had no idea what half of the machines were used for. Several moments went by, the clinking of glass and scraping of metal echoed off of the bare walls. The girl assumed that it was soundproof and all possible air leaks closed off with oxygen filtered in. He wasn't explaining as he said he would, but it really didn't surprise her that he had become distracted and had forgotten.

"Lay down." Leonardo finished with the vials and the machines ran without him; humming, buzzing, clicking. He motioned to the hospital bed across the room. She did as he asked and as soon as she did, he pressed a few buttons on the side of it and the bed began to vibrate and whirr. A circular panel slowly began to move around the bed, until the whole bed was encased in what reminded her of a toilet paper tube. Then it started making loud noises, some dull and some sharp. While she was waiting for Leo to finish his tests, she thought about a spaceship and what could have caused all of the sounds she was hearing. The casket stopped abruptly, and the panel slid back open, so fast that if she had sat up it might have taken her head off. Her host hadn't stuck around to help her up or even to say a word, as the data from the tube she'd been in must have been sent to a laptop in the lab area. Hope couldn't help but think he was still frustrated with her.

"Are you finding any answers?" Hope walked over to him and as she spoke, he turned to face her with an impatient, annoyed look painted on his face.

"The process takes a bit." He shook his head redirecting his focus to his work. Hope sat down, still scanning the room, but not wanting to get in Leo's way. When finally, he seemed finished, he turned his back on the table, leaving mess and all behind, with a frown over his face.

"Well...?" Hope asked him, curious and a bit concerned. Before answering her question, he placed his hand over his face and smeared it downward, as if trying to wipe the frustration away physically.

"It is precisely what I hypothesized would happen." Leo stated flatly. "In their arrogance and obsessive desire to drive forward in this war, they have made you into a Chimera."

"A Chimera?" She looked at her hands, as if somehow, they would be different. They weren't. "What do you mean a Chimera? She knew what the Greek version of a Chimera was, but she didn't seem to fit the description that had been portrayed in every historical depiction she had ever seen.

"A great many legends and myths are inaccurate. Intentionally so, to cause disbelief in the average human being. Some are not as easily fooled, some fold on blind faith alone." He led her back to the doorway they had come through when they walked in, once more getting a disinfecting spray down. When they were out of the room, he made his way back to the library, as it seemed to be where he spent the majority of his time. "It is not coincidence that a Chimera is depicted the way it is, consider for a moment, what a Chimera is composed of." He moved to a shelf, seeming to know exactly where to find what he was looking for. Thumbed through a few pages, then plopped the book down in front of her as they both sat. "The lion, the serpent, and the goat. Heaven is represented in this creature as the lion, God is king and always will be, just as the lion is king of the jungle. The serpent depicts humanity and creatures thereof, symbolized by original sin. The goat is an obvious reference to Baphomet, a prince that serves just below Lucifer in Hell. Asmodeus is also in that category. Princes, knights, whatever one wants to call them." Leo clasped his hands together, resting his elbows on the desk.

"So, what does that mean for me? Is that a good or a bad thing?" Hope wasn't exactly concerned, but she did feel uneasy as Leonardo pondered the question for several moments.

"I honestly do not know." This was not the answer she was looking for. "I have never seen one." Leo drifted off into story mode again. "See, a very, very long time ago, when the Earth was new, this war was far more gruesome than it is currently. That, I was not yet alive to see, but I do not wish for it to happen again." Hope had her eyes fixed on the sketches in the book, but still listened to the man as he spoke. "There are many unknowns, Heaven and Hell both have their own historical accounts. Our history began as our written languages became more established, you know it as The Holy Bible. Though, I have an immense problem with the current translations, they portray omitted and distorted accounts of history with omissions of important details. In any case, Heaven's book contains every account since the beginning of time and it continues to this day, they call it . The historical account of the opposite perspective, the Libro Sacro , contains the history, as per the abyss, beginning just beyond the war for Heaven. When Lucifer was cast out, the history of Hell began, this book is the reason we are in need of going to

Hell in the first place. We cannot get to Heaven, there is no known gate, Heaven comes to us. Our book, The Holy Bible does not have the information in it that we need to know to win this war, so we will need to access the information we lack in the Libro Sacro."

"So how are we supposed to be down there long enough to read the history of existence? There's no way I'm staying in Hell for long enough to read a whole book especially of the entire history of the world. I have seen the Bible; I can't even imagine what beyond that would even be like!" Hope was almost hyperventilating at this point.

"Relax, Gabriel took that into consideration. We just need to get close. I'll take care of the rest." Leo spoke matter-of-factly. "As far as your current state of being goes, there are very few that know what a Chimera is capable of and even fewer people that I would actually trust to know *about* your 'condition'. Some because they could not keep secrets and others, because they already have a horse in this race." Leo stood and put the book away. "Likely Sam is not high enough in command to send us or handle such matters and I have not the confidence in the Centrenarithan yet. So unfortunately, with our limited options, it looks as if we will need to make a trip back to see your new friend." Hope's eyes went instinctively wide when the words came out of his mouth, thankfully he'd had his back turned to her, putting the book back on the shelf. She silently cursed in her head at the thought of going with Leo to see Asmodeus. This plan was a disaster waiting to happen. It was the worst plan ever, but she didn't mention her feelings on this subject. If she did, Leonardo would know that there was something she was hiding from him. Even though The Architect had not staked a solid claim, his eyes sometimes gave away what emotions he truly held. So, there it was, back to the invisible building to make a deal with a devil. She smiled to herself when a thought popped into her head, something she dared not speak aloud. She giggled to herself thinking she would pack Leo's best fiddle in her purse. It was a silly joke referring to an old song, but sometimes humor was able to get her through tough situations.

The next day, when they reached the invisible building, Hope didn't even announce herself. She wanted to see if being able to open the door was a product of the demonic energy or if it was simply sealed to the outside in general. She grabbed the door and it swung open easily for her, Leo followed. She considered maybe sharing Asmodeus's energy gave her automatic admittance to the things he was able to get to. The receptionist was not at the desk, so Hope let herself in, remembering how to get to the demon's office from the lobby. Hope was nervous about how this interaction would go. It probably wasn't a great idea to bring Leo with her, but he had insisted that she not go alone this time. She was absolutely certain that Leonardo and Asmodeus already had a complicated relationship and not a single part of this situation was going to make it less so.

When they reached Deus's suite, she felt as if they were interrupting something as the door slid open in front of them. The demon's desk had been cleared since the last time she was here and, what she assumed, was some sort of ritualistic practice was spread out in front of him. He was obviously concentrating heavily on what he was doing, so much so that his eyes took on the darkness they had once before, with the faint red tint. He was mumbling words to himself, but Hope was surprised when he paused mid-Latin sentence to address them.

"I'll be with you in just a moment, business before pleasure." Asmodeus spoke, gesturing to some seating on the side of the room. Hope hadn't noticed it before, but then again, her attention had been a bit preoccupied. Asmodeus went back to what he was doing, beginning to also make extremely quick hand movements above his desk. Hope watched him and tried to commit to memory what he was doing. Before long, the hand movements began to form a red symbol within a glowing orb beneath them. It hung in the air, almost as if the friction between his hands and the air had caused his movements to catch on fire and had left a flaming stream of a tail. When the glow became satisfactory, he pulled one hand back, keeping the other still. Similar to having a dog on a leash, he held the glowing symbol still, remaining just as bright as it had been when he created it. With his free hand he pulled back, as if drawing a bow, only open palmed, fingers curled like he had a grip on the orb, even though this hand was the furthest from it. With one quick push of his free hand toward the figure, it was hurled toward the objects on his desk, shattering all around him. It seemed he had finished whatever it was he had been doing. His concentration he now redirected and made a move toward where Hope and Leo were waiting. "So...The Architect and Filia Dei , to what do I owe the pleasure?" He winked at Hope and frustration fell over Leo's face.

"We need to discuss a plan of action, in multiple regards. However, this discussion is best when all involved parties are present. It is obvious that Gabriel gave us all of the assistance he intended to, but the next part is up to us." Leo began.

"Alright, easy enough." Asmodeus leaned on a support beam, then snapped his fingers. "One moment." Without warning, Samael appeared as if the air had spat him out. He was only half dressed and true to the song he'd made up, held a bottle of whiskey in his hand. He seemed to be extremely surprised and a bit embarrassed when he realized where he was. "Now we're all here." Asmodeus seemed amused with Sam's reaction. Sam tossed him an angry glare.

After a while of Leo speaking and some brainstorming between the four, they came to the only logical decision they could, at least, considering the situation.

"I will be on the back end..." Asmodeus paused. "...open the door to the depths, give my assistance from behind the curtain..." He gave Leonardo a penetrating glance, then continued. "You can't go." He pointed to the angel. "...and you, well you're just supernaturally 'gifted', at the moment. Other than accompanying The Architect, you're just not extremely useful yet, dulcedo ."

Hope wouldn't have considered herself useless, she knew a few things, but she kept quiet, because in this particular plan, she was more of a liability than a benefit, but Leo couldn't go alone. Even though Sam was Fallen, he was still an angel, and he would be noticed quickly, blowing their cover, especially with the Holy juice Gabriel had given him. Asmodeus had to keep up appearances, he seemed to be with them, but Hope continuously questioned his motives. He was after all a demon. He'd told her that he had given her the energy so as to stay protected, but something didn't quite sit right. While it may have been a partial truth, Hope was almost sure that he likely had other motives as well.

Asmodeus took what looked similar to an oversized Bingo dauber, out of a refrigerator within the room. In that moment, Hope noticed that there were actually two fridges in the very large office space, except the one he had taken the utensil out of had held a lock and wards on it. Hope was curious, but not so much so that she would ask about it at this moment.

The demon moved toward an empty wall and began to paint symbols in a deep crimson liquid. Hope convinced herself that it was just acrylic paint, but deep down she knew exactly what it was. When he was finished with what seemed like some sort of spell-work, he took a single step backward. Reaching out toward the wall, he placed his fingertips in the center of the circle he'd created, and as he did so the symbols began to glow. When he began to pull back, his fingers came together on the wall, as if he were grabbing something. The wall within the circle became malleable, and she could see it waver beneath his hand. Then, almost as if he were tightly grasping a blanket that had been on the wall, instead of the wall itself, he began to pull. His grip was so tight that his pale knuckles almost became a blue-white. She could barely see by watching the profile of his face, but the strain of this endeavor caused the fiery glow she'd seen in his eyes previously to ignite into a full blaze, consuming almost every part of them. The fire was so strong that Hope could have sworn that it would somehow escape him and burn the building to the ground. The whole while Hope could feel a tingling sensation in her veins and the pentagram on the left side of her body began to pulse with a similar red luminescence. The harder he pulled on the wall, the stronger the fire inside of him grew and the more the red within her own body grew. However, instead of the explosion she had expected, Hope watched as a single brilliant tear, similar to lava, started to trail down his cheek. It wasn't long after that the wall finally gave in. With a pop loud enough to cause their ears to ring, the center of the circle became a dark portal, the ring around it continuing to shine fire red. Asmodeus having let go when it broke open, turned to address Leo and Hope. He was exhausted and his body slowly put out the fire his eyes had contained. The only part of the biological process his body had been through that didn't begin to go away immediately, was a scorch mark left behind from the lava tear. Even the brilliance of Hope's own energy began to die down.

"This will get you there. I have a few allies on the other side but stay cautious." He paused turning to Leonardo. "When you need to return, it will be in your hands. The portal is open and protected on this side, but the other side is something else entirely." Hope and Leo nodded in agreement. "If you are discovered down there, which is likely, there are some that might help." He took a small piece of paper out of his pocket and handed it to Da Vinci. "These are the names of those who might help you...but remember, they also might not. Be prepared."

Leonardo unfolded it and quickly committed it to memory, likely a part of his own gift from Gabriel.

"Also...you can't go in there like that." Deus motioned toward the whole of Leo. Hope could see how tired the demon was as he made his way back to the fridge with the lock. He pulled a small case out and walked back to Leo. "You stick out like a sore thumb. You know what you need to do." Leo took the case from him, opening it, and glancing over the contents. The contents of the case could have passed for that of a diabetic, but the clear glass bottle had no label. It had to be the demon venom that Leo had told her about. Gabriel had told him that he wouldn't need it anymore in order to remain of useful age. However, this was different entirely. Now they were in need of going 'undercover'. His human energy might be noticed. They couldn't take that chance. "To stay off their radar, you have to seem as if you belong. Hope has received my blessing, but you will need a little camouflage, you know how long you have until it wears off, make every moment count."

Leonardo looked at the case with disdain, as if when it would bite him. The emotion transferred to Asmodeus. Hope hung onto the word 'blessed'. He spoke it as if it were normal. She hadn't considered that blessings could work both ways, but she supposed that was the easiest way to describe it.

"I understand. There is no need to dig that hole any deeper." It came out almost like a snarl and Da Vinci moved toward what seemed to be a bathroom. After a few moments of waiting, the man came back out, though Hope could see a difference in him. His yellow, sparkling aura was now a tarnished coppery orange. He seemed to be in a foul mood about it, but he did seem to have an extra jolt of energy in his steps. He glared at Deus for one more moment, before turning his gaze to Hope. "Are you ready?" The question was rhetorical, whereas saying no wasn't really an option. At the same time, her nervousness and anxiety refused to allow even a squeak of her voice to pass through her vocal cords, so she just nodded in agreement and took the hand that Leo 0offered to her as they stepped into the portal. From this point forward, they were on their own. Two humans, a world full of demons and the damned...what could go wrong?

9

Hope had expected fire and chains, at the very least, howls of pain and agony. Instead, what she was met with was a long dark hallway. It was so long that she couldn't see the other end. She looked toward Leo, who didn't seem to miss a step, walking forward instinctively. Sometimes it amazed her just how brave he was, maybe it wasn't bravery, but it certainly seemed that way. She wanted to grab his hand and stand behind him the whole way, but she figured that might come off as weak, which wouldn't be beneficial to this particular quest. He might not have been nervous, but she couldn't help feeling on edge, especially with everything she had heard throughout her life about the place.

She hadn't seen the paper that Leonardo had, of course even if she had, it likely wouldn't have made a difference. There was no way she would have been able to remember it, especially in that short amount of time. She wanted to ask him who they were looking for, but she was afraid to break the silence of the hallway. Their light steps seemed to echo off of the walls as if there were no other sounds in this particular world.

In the low light, she couldn't see much detail, she couldn't even see exactly where the light was coming from. It was almost as if it didn't come from anywhere, it *just was.* This was a concept that she kept rolling around in her mind, trying to figure out where the light came from, though it was really just something to focus on. Every few feet, on either side of the hallway, there were doors. The doors were solid metal, without windows. None of them had a doorknob, instead they seemed to have a pressure plate. Each had a plaque with symbols etched into them, all with different 'writing'. She was afraid to use her sight to read it down here, not wanting to draw any unnecessary attention in their direction.

Suddenly behind them there was the loud noise of a heavy door closing. Hope almost jumped onto Leonardo's back, startled by the loud sound. It bounced off of the walls, recreating the sound over and over until it faded out. They were immediately discovered and seemingly apprehended.

"Quid tu hic agis ?" The unknown entity was taller than both she and Leo, completely enshrouded in a dark-colored cloak. It was impossible in this lighting to tell exactly what color the cloak was, but from what she could see, it wasn't completely black. She blinked, trying to look beyond the hood. She wasn't sure what to expect, but what came next was the furthest thing she could have thought of. "Quid tu hic agis ?" It repeated itself, the voice was more like a reverberation than an -actual- voice. Its hands reached up to the hood and pulled it back. As it did so, the darkness beneath the hood gave way to a face. The face was so familiar that it set her aback and her eyes went wide. She glanced toward

Leo. Her companion also seemed to be shocked at the face of the creature, though he hid his reaction much better than she did, and soon recovered his full composure. Likely whatever this creature was, Leo had a book about it. His unsaid opinion was partly matter of fact, but likely, in part out of annoyance. Hope, over the last few days, had begun to feel perturbed by Leonardo's know-it-all attitude and it grinded on her nerves. She knew it wasn't likely intentional, but she couldn't help feeling the way she felt about it. Of course, in his defence, if anyone was entitled to justified arrogance it would be Da Vinci. The man literally helped build the world into what it was today, the father of modern innovation.

"Nos sunt hic ad armata Megaera quaedam de opinione citius intercepti." The Architect spoke the words without flaw, as if he had been speaking the language his entire life. The creature, who currently looked like her Great Uncle Gregory, simply nodded and walked past them into the darkness. She had thought he was going to keep going, but instead his creepy cataracted eyes turned back toward them. He made her feel uncomfortable, when her uncle was alive, he had given her a similar feeling. She had always just gotten a weird vibe from him. Hope was fairly sure this creature wasn't her uncle, not that he might not be in Hell, but the way Leo had reacted to the creature made her think that maybe it looked differently to each person that saw it.

"Sequere ." The creature said to them, beginning to make its way into the dark hallway toward the direction of the door he had come in through. However, he moved past it. The creature left its hood down and though she couldn't see its feet, it seemed to be gliding without touching the floor.

Hope and Leo followed. They had no idea where they were going, making sure to stay cautious and ready for anything. At the same time, they assumed that their new acquaintance was leading them in the right direction. The creature, although seeming suspicious of them at first, did not seem to be concerned any longer. After all, Hope figured it would take a moron to walk right into Hell and start a fight. Kicking a hornet's nest would likely be safer.

After what seemed like forever following the creature, he turned toward one of the doors and reached out to the pressure plate. Chills went down Hope's spine as she watched the creature begin to open the door. When she saw the Gregory-faced person's hand reach out, it was merely a shadow. There was no skin, no bone, just a shadow that pressed the button in. It didn't open immediately, instead a noticeable red light began to grow, through the transparent, shadow hand and with it the creature spoke some words. She assumed it was something similar to a magic spell that locked and unlocked the door.

"Ut ostium crinem solvere ingredi. " The door made a clicking noise, before it popped open with a slightly louder noise echoing through the hall again. He only partially opened the door and did not enter it, at least not yet. Instead, he directed his words to whatever or whoever was on the other side. "Megaera veniam sunt externis theatrum petens. " After a few moments, the creature seemed to have gotten permission to allow them in, it opened the door wide, allowed them inside, and closed the door behind them. It stayed in the hallway instead of entering with them, it seemed if he realized that his mission was now complete.

When the two humans were completely inside, their eyes moved around the 'room'. In true Leo style, he seemed unimpressed. In complete contrast, Hope was in awe of everything she saw. They hadn't entered a room per say, it actually seemed as if they were outside. The air was warm, crisp, and sweet. It smelled of flowers and fruit. Regardless of which direction she looked, she was surrounded by green foliage, dotted with the colors of spring, and a blue sky. It was in this moment, Hope realized that the door had disappeared behind them. The new development sent fear coursing through her, if anything went wrong, they had no way out.

Hope turned her head back and forth much too quickly to seem calm and collected. She felt claustrophobic, even though the area looked like a beautiful garden, it felt like she had just stepped into a cage. She was unsure how she knew everything in this place was an elaborate illusion, she just did. She attributed it to the paranormal energies that now inhabited her body. She inspected her surroundings thoroughly. It reminded her of pictures and videos she'd seen of ancient Greece, before being damaged by time. It was truly beautiful, even if it did make her nervous.

"I understand you're looking for me?" A feminine voice with reverberation, similar to the hallway creature's, flowed in waves toward them. Though, obviously there was a slight difference. The voice seemed to have other voices behind it, as if there were several people speaking at the same time, but Hope knew it was only one. This woman must have been on the list Asmodeus had given Leo. For now, Hope kept silent, as Megaera appeared from behind a broken pillar. The woman was beautiful to the naked eye, though they couldn't yet know exactly what the woman's true form looked like. Megaera quickly caught on that Hope wasn't exactly what she seemed, and she narrowed her eyes on the girl. The scantily clad woman studied Hope, without directing her attention to Leonardo yet. Long, brown ringlets bounced as the woman moved toward her. "I know who he is, but you are new." Quite suddenly she addressed Leo, without moving her eyes away from Hope. "You created a Chimera?!" Meg took a deep breath. "It's starting, isn't it?" Her head snapped quickly toward Leo. "I knew they were saving you to play a part of whatever would bring on the Apocalypse. It wasn't if, just when." She rolled her eyes and moved away from Hope. She sat down on the base of a broken statue. "So, what do you want from me?" Without waiting for an answer, she seemed to catch wind of something in the air. She took a deep breath and closed her eyes, as if she were trying to smell something. "That explains it. The bastard would send you to me, wouldn't he?" She now seemed irked by her thoughts. "What is it you want and why would Asmodeus send you to me?"

"You're not friends?" Hope piped up in a small voice, confused as to why the Demonic Knight would send them to an individual he was not on good terms with. Meg shrugged her shoulders.

"We have a history, it ended badly, but I wouldn't murder him on sight, if that is what you're asking." She paused. "Though, I suppose he hasn't many allies here anymore." Leo chimed in at this.

"It was a short list; you were simply at the beginning." His words were dry and all business. "We're here to see 'the book'. We were told you or one of the others on this list might be able to get us there." Meg's jilted love affair did not seem to interest him in the slightest.

"The Libro Sacro?" Meg laughed sarcastically. "You want me to get you into the most guarded place in Hell, so that you can read a book? For, Lucy's sake, I haven't even read the *quite literally* damned book." She paused just long enough for Leo to almost begin to reply, but she spoke over him. "I understand the importance, especially right now, but Admon is not going to let you near it, let alone give you an Abyss Public Library card."

"Hell has a library?" Hope let a thought slip through her vocal cords, before realizing that Megaera was probably being sarcastic. Megaera behaved as if she hadn't even heard the question.

"There are others on the list. I'm sure Asmodeus had a plan and considered his resources here in a calculated fashion." Leo responded. The woman shrugged.

"The Architect and a Filia Dei walk into a bar…" Megaera shook her head. "Alright, fine. We will round up a posse and rob Firmamentum est ad Inferos …at this point, what have I got to lose, I suppose?" She sighed. "So, I get the *princess's* investment in this endeavor, but yours Da Vinci? What makes you tick, sweet cheeks?" The two followed Meg back to 'her home'. It was odd walking through the outdoors, then into a medium sized house, while knowing that they were technically still inside of a single room. Hope had almost forgotten several times since she'd been here. Once they reached the inside, Hope moved around, while still listening to the conversation. It seemed the woman was just making small talk, but Hope was sure Leo would consider every word he spoke to her carefully before he said it. Unlike herself, the man had much more verbal control in situations like this.

"It is a long story." Leonardo replied, an uncomfortable look growing on his face. Hope had gotten a strong impression that this topic was something he had wanted left alone. She'd had enough respect for the man that she'd let the issue go, though she wasn't sure that Meg was the type of creature that would. Though, one of the things the conversation between the two speaking did help with, it distracted the woman for long enough to take a peek with her newly acquired vision. Even though she made it quick, she wasn't sure if it would be noticed or felt without seeing it. A mere moment was long enough for Hope to see everything she needed to, but even that mere moment seemed to have been noticed.

"You know, if you're going to do that, you might want to hide your signature a bit better." The woman didn't seem to be concerned with rudeness like Ja'Hari had. "Unless..." She paused, squinting her eyes and shaking her head. "You don't know how, do you?" She turned back toward Leo. "You're telling me, you brought her down here, not only a Chimera, but also a Filia Dei, into Hell, and she doesn't even know how to hide her energy footprint?"

"We didn't have time for her to learn in a conventional way." Leo's tone remained calm, but his expression gave away what he was feeling. Though Hope couldn't be sure whether he was frustrated with the woman for taking so long or because of the complicated situation they were currently in.

"No wonder Deus sent you to me first." More quickly than

Hope could even process thoughts of protest, the woman rushed her and shoved her palm hard on the girl's sternum. The movement knocked the wind out of Hope and caused her to take a step back. It didn't hurt, but it felt as if she was hit by an extremely strong gust of wind all at once. "There, it won't work for everything, but it will work for most."

"What did you do?" Hope asked her, she would ask questions about what the woman's true form eventually, but the girl structured her inquiries in order of their importance.

"Energy...gives off a signal, specific to each *type* of creature, but not just that, each *individual* creature." She spoke with her hands, almost like she was explaining to a ten-year-old. "Each specific genus and species of creature has different amounts of distance before they are able to pick up on those energies and discern their origin, almost like a scent." She moved to sit down, at least while she was explaining things. "For someone like myself, it's a few feet. For someone like Arassmas'en, the individual that brought you to me, it is almost impossible to get close enough for him to see that energy, which is also why he wasn't suspicious. Patrolling the hallways is not his job, so he doesn't need that ability. Lucifer and Sanctus Mater likely already know you're here, but they're also unlikely to bother. If the other Knights and higher ranked Demons do not know you're here already, they will soon enough. The inscription I placed on your chest plate will help, but the sooner you're able to control what's been given to you to add to that, the sooner you will be completely off radar. You reek of angel...masked by knight, but the holy presence of your energy is unmistakable here. It is likely, as you learn more about your new gifts, you will also gain the ability to sense nearby energies, though your range is currently unknown. A surviving chimera is not a normal situation."

"All radar? Or just Hell's?" Hope asked fairly sure, at this point, by the end of this war, her whole body was going to be a religious relic.

"All radar. Except for those whose energies you share." She answered. Hope simply nodded, before she moved on with the conversation. "No known magic can hide you from those bound to you...which, in your case, could be both a good and a bad thing."

"So, the creature we met in the hallway, what was he? And you, you're one of the fallen?" Hope had seen her wings with the sight, they weren't like Gabriel's, and they certainly weren't clipped like Samael's had been. Hope was curious because she had been under the impression that during the fall God had removed their wings as a mark of shame. No one had told her, but having seen Sam's amputated appendages, she had figured it to be a good bet that they were all similar. Yet Megaera's wings, instead of glowing, had almost produced a void in the red aura that surrounded her; she could see red light, but it was as if the woman's wings were an emptiness, not an appendage. Meg chuckled lightly.

"Not so much." Meg seemed to pause in order to decide how she wanted to answer that question. "I was. Then I wasn't. Then...I suppose you could call me a Hell's Angel." She shrugged, obviously realizing the joke she made by the smirk on her face. "I'm a Fury. It's a long story, but ultimately, I chose a side, my side lost. The wings are a participation trophy. Angels that fought for Heaven kept the white, fluffy, corporal appendages as a badge of honor. Angels who rebelled against Heaven, myself included, were torn from the only home we'd ever known and thrown to the Earth. However, not without a parting gift. Our wings were broken and cut, all of us, and considering you have Sam's energy, I'm sure you have seen the aftermath first-hand. Lucifer considered those who hadn't chosen a side, like Samael, lacking the ability to be trusted, unsure what they might do in order to regain God's favor. Those who chose to be Legionnaires for Lucifer, were given the choice to remain on Earth or to live in...what *he* called a 'new paradise'. Having been banished from my home and feeling out of place within your home, I decided to follow Lucifer in order to assist with building what you see here. I was given the wings and my place within the ranks for exemplary work within this dimension." She made air quotes with her hands. "You see, humans don't exactly understand Lucy, you all think he's this evil, disfigured being that spouts nothing but lies and forces people to commit sin against God. It just isn't true. Lucifer is the greatest salesman that has ever existed. He is beautiful and alluring. He is incapable of lies, originally having been an angel we are not hard wired that way...plus, he doesn't need to. Human nature is to sin, sometimes they just need a small push in the right direction. Lucifer, Sanctus Mater, the Knights, myself, and other demonic creatures cannot create or force sin from scratch. The sin is already there, sometimes it just needs a little coaxing to come out in the open. I won't say that we are innocent, we are what we are. We all have a place in the larger picture, ours is to simply reveal the unworthy." She crossed her legs, seeming almost as if she were finished with her story. "Oh yes, and Arassmas'en, he is Alû . If you were wondering, you see what your mind tells you to see. Alû produce a hormone that causes anyone who looks directly at them to see an individual that would bring out feelings of uneasiness. It works out well for their purposes."

Hope pondered what the woman had said for a little while. There seemed to be so many different versions of the same story. She assumed the book would give a less telephone-esque version of everything. This thought led her to the ultimate question, would the meaning of life be in Hell's book? Even though she couldn't walk right into Heaven, she wondered if the answer to the eternal question was in it. Of course, she also supposed that the answer might actually be in the Bible and humans were just not looking hard enough. She made a promise to herself to reread the book when they got out of here...if she and Leonardo made it out alive, that is.

10

Megaera conjured the hidden door out of her room easily, as this reality seemed to have been made for her specifically. Hope was sure others could open it from the inside as well, but it probably would have taken them much more effort. Stepping out into the hallway, Meg stopped just outside the door.

"Who's next on the list?" The woman asked Leo casually. However, Leonardo was once again being interrupted before he could get out an answer, there was a sudden foul smell that caused the humans to cover their nose and mouth. The strong smell of fire and sulfur hung heavy in the air. Hope searched the area around them with her eyes, trying to figure out where the odor was coming from. Out of the corner of her eye, she thought she saw something move. She aligned her vision with it, but she couldn't see anything. "Some things down here you won't be able to see with your human eyes. Take a look. Quickly, no one is close enough to see, but let's not take many chances." Hope looked at her, before flipping her supernatural switch. She was beginning to get much better at turning it off and on, which wasn't a huge accomplishment, but at least it was something.

The glow of the energy within Hope began to build quickly around her, however unlike the other times she'd used it, the merging of energies was now noticeable. The girl's aura had now shifted from white, to blue, and now...shades of purple, blended with blues and reds on either side. It seemed to take all three of them by surprise, so much so that Hope had almost forgotten the reason for turning it on in the first place. When her eyes finally fell on the creature that had been invisibly following them in the hallway, she couldn't help but smile. Sitting on the floor in front of her was the largest puppy she had ever seen.

She could see him as if she were looking at him through infrared. He gave off a red glow in her gifted sight and his body seemed to be created of a material similar to the Fury's wings. As he was seated on the floor, the pup's head was taller than her knees, from the way he was currently built and the happy playful expression on his face he couldn't have been very old, a couple of months at the most, which left Hope concerned about how big this creature might actually get. She wasn't nervous about the young one in front of her, as he seemed to want her to play with him, she was worried about the full-size parents of the creature. Hope knelt down to pet the invisible baby, however just a pet wasn't exactly what the little guy had in mind. As soon as she was crouched down, the creature plowed into her with force, though it was far from malicious. It was simply a large dog who had no idea how large he actually was. Hope lost her balance and ended up sitting on the floor scratching and petting the pup.

"They're not supposed to be roaming the hallway, this one must have gotten loose." Magaera reached toward the animal and gave it a quick pat. "We've had quite a few litters born lately, now that I know the next phase of the war is here, it makes sense that the hounds would breed more in preparation. They are more native to Vorago than we are."

"He's such a sweet little thing, I thought things here are supposed to be scary?" Hope had let the vision fade, but as the little dog moved around, she could see that the hallway was a bit distorted around the hound.

"The big ones are, but it is also up for debate, as it is with most creatures, whether nature or nurture plays more of a part in their eventual personality. The dogs seem more comfortable here and have been raised under purposeful training, testing the theory is next to impossible. If one of the grown hounds wants something, they tend to get it. There are few creatures and beings here that can take on a hound and come out of it still standing." Meg paused. "It's not invisibility, you know. It's camouflage, like a chameleon. They are flesh and blood, unlike a lot of things here, they are likely one of the most innocent creatures in Hell but trained for violence. They also choose their master and that choice, to them, is *for life.*"

Hope stopped petting the pup, who had rolled over on his back, feeling the weight of his large body in her lap, completely enjoying the tummy rubs that he was receiving. Her face went white as a ghost, and she lost all expression while looking toward the woman.

"What does that mean? He was following us...he was

following me!" Hope looked down surprised toward the invisible weight in her lap. "How am I supposed to know how to take care of a Hellhound?"

"I'm sure you'll figure it out. If not, Asmodeus is on your plane, he can help." The two women seemed to be completely ignoring the fact that Da Vinci was even there.

"Now wait just a minute, we are not bringing a Hellhound to our world, let alone into our home. It is my home and I choose not to step in piles of invisible dog fences while walking around *my home*." Leo began shaking his head fervently. "No. Absolutely not. We have a mission, we need to stay on task, we have a time limit." Hope had made up her mind, she was taking the young pup with them whether he liked it or not, but she remembered Asmodeus mentioning Da Vinci needed to hurry. "He could be useful." She knew her best chance at getting him to agree wasn't by pulling on his heartstrings. The best way to get him on her side was to be logical with him. She flashed the vision long enough to push the pup away so she could stand up. "When he's bigger, he will be useful in this fight. Until then, think about what you could learn from him. I'm sure a native creature of Hell could give great insight to the world itself." She was starting to figure him out, proven even more when he narrowed his eyes on her, then moved his gaze to the empty air beside her containing the creature in question.

"Very well." He sighed. "However, until I create something to see the animal and its leavings, it is up to you to handle and learn of its care." Da Vinci then turned his gaze toward Meg, seeming to almost treat Hope like she was a child in that moment. "Shall we proceed? The next on the list is Veranon."

"Ver-..." Meg seemed to be confused for a moment, she seemed to recognize the name, but at the same time tried to figure out why Asmodeus might put the individual on the list. However, it wasn't long before she shook her head and rolled her eyes. "Alright. This way." She started walking in the direction they had been moving before and she seemed to assume that they would follow her, so she didn't look back, even when she spoke to them. "Leonardo, contain yourself with this one. Hope, keep your familiar close. Veranon can be 'overwhelming' to some."

"Overwhelming?" Hope repeated in a questioning fashion. Leo seemed suspicious, but still assured of himself, as always. Though, he remained quiet.

"Yes." Meg paused, trying to decide what she was going to say. "It seems our mutual acquaintance might have given you a laundry list of past entanglements. It seems possible by the first two names on his list, that the short list of those he trusts, is likely to be those he has bedded in the past." She stopped short, turning quickly, her eyes seeming to pierce Hope's soul for a moment, suspiciously. Hope stopped just in time to avoid running into her, eyes going wide at the accusatory gaze that the other woman gave to her.

"I promise you, that is not the case with *all* allies he has right now." Hope spoke it like a confession, though within it, she felt a slight pang of guilt at what *had* actually happened, even if it hadn't been a free action on her part.

"Hmm...I suppose not." Oddly enough, the Fury seemed

protective over the Knight, almost as if she still held feelings for him. They turned and again continued on. "Vera has an effect on people and if you're not careful, it can be more than many can handle. For a normal human, it would be almost impossible, for you..." She paused her speech, but not her steps. "It will be interesting to see what happens, I suppose."

When it seemed to Hope that they had been walking for hours through a hallway where one door seemed almost the same as the next, with merely the symbols on the plaques as a difference, Meg lifted her hand to a specific door. The air around her hand wavered, as if it were radiating heat and she pressed in the door plate. Unlike the creature that had opened her door, she didn't announce herself or ask for permission to open the door widely. As they made their way through the door, Hope understood why. It wasn't a room like Meg's had been, to Hope's frustration, it was another hallway. This one was different, it was much grander, something the girl imagined might have been in a medieval castle.

"She's here. We two do not get along, so you are on your own." She looked to Leonardo. "Who is next on our list? I will see to them, then we shall come back together when the recruits are made." It wasn't a suggestion, Meg was telling them what she intended on doing, without regards to any plans they might have. Hope still wasn't sure she trusted the woman, but at this point, she trusted Meg more than Deus.

"Aēshma." The man recited the next name off of his mental list. Megaera nodded her head, seeming to confirm of her theory, as the expression on her face seemed to convey.

"Of course," She took a few steps in the direction that they had come from. "It may take a while and likely you will need to find me, especially you…" She addressed Hope. "I under-stand Asmodeus's plan now. Win Vera to our side, Aēshma won't be difficult, we were once friends." From the way she said this, it seemed like there was some unsaid history concerning the situation. It wasn't long before the woman disappeared from view and the two humans were left alone in the luxurious hallway…Hope, Leonardo, and the rollie Hellhound pup .

Leo walked through the door first, followed by Hope, then the young Hellhound. This particular moment turned out to be the most terrifying moment that Hope had ever experienced. They had stepped through the door into vast nothingness. Hope stood suspended and all around her seemed like the night sky, but the stars seemed closer. They dotted the area around the two on all sides. There was no sun, no moon, no Earth…just the darkness of space dimly lit, but enough to see each other clearly. It wasn't actually outer space, because they could breathe and they seemed to be anchored to something by gravity, which meant everything was likely an illusion. Both she and Leonardo, searched the area for signs of life within the twinkling stars.

"It is beautiful, isn't it?" A voice came from nowhere and almost directly after a pocket seemed to open up against the scenery. "You're not who I expected. What is your business here?" The woman walked toward them, lighting up a red, electric pathway as she moved. It was almost as if the woman was the power source of this room. Much as Asmodeus's eyes contained fire, this woman's eyes sparked with red lightning. In fact, her whole body surged with energy. As she came closer, she stared at Hope. "You reek of 'Deus and I see you've brought a pet." Even though they knew the woman was speaking, her lips did not move, and her voice seemed to come from all around them. Hope could feel the large baby pressed against the back of her legs, small whimpers escaping him here and there. The creature seemed nervous of the woman. Hope didn't speak, once again Leo spoke up.

"We were given a list of individuals that might help us with our objective here." He didn't go into detail but hoped he did not have to give her any more information.

"Oh, sweet cheeks, I rarely help anyone with anything. I'm not sure what Asmodeus told you, but we have a history..." She rolled her eyes.

"Every individual on the list seems to. This is much more important than a past lovers quarrel." Leonardo spoke almost like a politician trying to build a foreign alliance. The woman was hard to read, as her face was emotionless, and electricity crackled around her in her silence. In response, she raised her hands, as if she were reaching out to the two of them, however just when they might have felt the woman's touch, Hope's world went dark.

When Hope awoke, she blinked a few times, sitting up and looking around her. Her eyes fell on a familiar sight, she was in her apartment. As if she had been sleeping, the world she had become a part of suddenly seemed like just a bad dream. Beside her, she felt a weight padding up to her, her cat began to comfort her as he had so many times before when she'd had a bad dream. Her mind swirled with what she now questioned whether they were memories or fantasies. Her hands ran over her chest where the two symbols had been. It was an odd feeling, her skin was smooth, but a part of her felt as if something was missing. She got out of bed, wandering about the apartment, inspecting things in order to make up her mind about what was real and what was not. It was tempting to just accept this as reality and reject everything that her mind told her had happened. It would be so much easier to go back to the life she'd had before. The life where she was ignorant, but that ignorance made her feel safe. The life where the biggest responsibilities she had was to keep a job and take care of her cat. She plopped down on her couch, her eyes moving to the window which had played a big part in the last memory that she'd had of this apartment. She remembered the monstrous floating jellyfish that had tried to pull her out of the window. Did she just imagine it? After a moment, Set hopped up onto her lap, rubbing up against her, trying to get her to pet him. Hope looked down, placing both hands on the sides of his soft black face.

"What do you think, Set? Should we just stay here?" She took a deep breath, as she asked the rhetorical questions. "It would be a lot easier to stay here..." Her mind drifted for a few moments, but the pat of a paw on the side of her face brought her back. She looked back down to Set, staring into his bright yellow eyes. Something about his eyes seemed different and as she kept her gaze fixed on his in something of a staring contest, the world around them seemed to waver and become fuzzy. The illusion faltered, like a standing pool that someone had thrown a rock into. Then it began to fade away, back to the starry sky that they had walked into. Hope wasn't sure what the woman had done, but she knew that it was with the intention of testing them to see what tolerance the two had. Likely it was for this reason Meg did not want to come in and had warned them about the woman. Hope had assumed when Meg had said to keep her familiar close that she had been speaking of the pup, who was still beside her, seeming concerned, but it was Set that brought her back, her anchor to reality as it would seem. Set was eleven years old, and he had been in Hope's life for ten of them, they had been through so much together that she couldn't even imagine being without him. Her mind momentarily flashed a concern for his well-being, considering he was on Earth, and she was in Hell. However, she was sure that the large, old house that he had free roam of likely had mice to keep him entertained. She reassured herself that he would be alright for a couple of days. It was then that she remembered Leonardo. Without directing her attention to Veranon, she focused on him.

Da Vinci's eyes were open, but glazed over, as if his body was frozen in place, but his mind was somewhere else. Red electricity crackled around him, as if it held him captive within it. She frantically studied the situation, unsure as to what to do, but ultimately deciding to grab him. She was going to try to pull him out of the daze, but what actually happened, was something that she couldn't have predicted.

Again, Hope was thrown into darkness, opening her eyes to a foreign world, a world she had only heard about, never having dreamed that she might experience it. Everything was dirty and archaic. Technology was non-existent, but sketches of devices and designs far beyond the time period she seemed to be in were scattered about. Once a mess, always a mess, she supposed. She knew where she was. She had been in an illusion of a world that she was most comfortable, so this must have been a time period where he felt most at home. She made her way around the stone building taking in the scenery with amazement. She found him fervently writing at a desk and as she walked closer to him, he noticed and turned to look at her. As he did so, the expression on his face was one she had never seen him give her before. It was almost as if he gave her the same expression, she'd seen him give his work; passionate, determined, intrigued, and excited. She'd rarely ever seen him with such a look since she met him, let alone when he looked at her.

"Lisabetta . I did not expect you, my lady." He spoke as if he had done so a thousand times. The man slid his arms around her, and she seemed to fit perfectly there, as if she had been made for this embrace. Hope didn't feel herself at this moment though and it was obvious that Leo didn't see her as who she was on the inside, he saw the illusion of what Veranon wanted him to see. Before she could protest, the embrace turned into a kiss and as much as she knew it was a complicated situation, she not only allowed it, but instinctively matched his intensity. The kiss was unlike anything she'd ever felt before. It was unlike when he'd kissed her before, it was unlike when she had kissed Asmodeus, it was unlike when she had kissed Sam. Hope wasn't sure if it was because she was the illusion of someone Da Vinci had been in love with or because this time period was before he had become jaded by life. For a few moments, she almost wished she could stay in this illusion, after all it *was* much better than hers had been. It might not have been familiar or her own life, but it was romantic and enticing. The kiss was deep, and it lasted much longer than Hope had expected it to. When it did end, the two stood together, their faces so close that they could feel each other's breath on their still damp lips. The warmth between them was hard to ignore and it begged to induce more primitive urges. Hope pulled away, knowing that allowing it to go any further would be wrong.

"Leonardo." Even her voice was not her own in this moment, masked by the illusion of another woman. In this illusion, Hope's mind was her own, but he didn't see her, he saw Lisabetta. "You are dreaming, Leonardo. This is not real."

"Reality is the true illusion, my love. The perception of one world versus another, the ability to see light over darkness, color over the dull and dim." He reached out to her. "If this is but a dream, why not choose to keep dreaming, over what was once a nightmare?" He had a point, but Hope knew she had to bring him out of it, back to the battle they were fighting and gaining knowledge from the Libro Sacro. It was a responsibility they had accepted and were expected to follow through. The whole world was depending on them.

"Leonardo, we must continue, for the good of all. We must not lose focus on our purpose. We must not lose ourselves. We must not give in." Hope stood watching him, as the same expression remained on his face. He once again closed the gap she had put between them and embraced her.

"The world can wait...*Hope.*" For a second time he kissed her, this kiss was similar to the last, but there was something a bit different about it, she knew this kiss was actually meant for her and not the other woman. He had spoken her name when he kissed her this time. He saw Hope through the illusion. As she opened her eyes and the kiss ended, she found herself back in the starlit room. Leo still held her, and she looked into his eyes now with her own, the magic now having faded. He let her go abruptly and there was a few seconds of awkwardness between them, as he knew she had seen a part of him that he hadn't yet shown her. Neither seemed to know exactly how to react to what had just happened. Hope took a few steps backward, eyes still focused on him for a few moments.

"How disappointing." The voice of Vera echoed around them once again and they both searched the area for the woman. "By the look of it, the Architect's vision was shaping up to be quite the encounter. On the other hand, our young chimera's was quite boring. You really should put yourself out there more."

"Enough." Da Vinci seemed to become frustrated, filing what had just happened away for a later time. "We are not here for your games. We are not here for your entertainment. We are here because we need to get to *the book.* Will you help us or not?" He was forceful toward the woman, demanding her attention and the seriousness of the situation. The woman's response to him wasn't a pleasant one, instead she seemed to become defensive.

"What do I get out of this deal and what is it that you want of me?" The woman asked, seeming to take a seat in the emptiness, especially considering the room didn't appear to have any true structure to it.

"You get me." A voice came from behind the two humans, the voice of Megaera. "You've been wanting a face off against me for a very long time, Vera. I think it's time you had it, but not until you get us past Admon." Veranon seemed to be intrigued by the proposal and cracked a small smile that seemed out of place on her face.

"Alright, so what is the plan then?" The red lightning in Vera's eyes seemed brighter and fiercer.

11

Hope took a deep breath, blinking and nervous about the plan they'd come up with. Da Vinci hadn't said there were any other names on the list, but she thought that maybe he was holding out, considering the controversial nature of the current members of their party. When Meg had entered Veranon's room, she had been followed by another woman that Hope assumed to be Aēshma. The woman was quiet and much taller and broader than even Da Vinci, Hope estimated that she was nearly seven foot tall, if not taller. She wore plain clothing, almost masculine, compared to the other two women. Megaera's attire was very Greek in nature, Vera's clothes were much more revealing with almost a prehistoric aspect to them, though they appeared of high quality. It made Hope think that at one time, Vera might have been worshipped by ancient peoples. She was impressive in what she could do and how she appeared. Hope still didn't quite understand why they needed so much help going up against a single man. Hope understood that this man was likely powerful, but after all, it was just one guard. She didn't even think that Leonardo understood the reasons why the five of them were needed, but he apparently trusted that Asmodeus was steering him in the right direction and that he had much more knowledge of the inner workings of Hell than most.

"How do I look?" Hope took a couple of steps backward. Meg had taught her a quick trick and Hope focused hard at forcing the demonic energy to overrule and encase her form. At this moment, Hope did not look like Hope. On the side-lines, Veranon worked her illusion magic, giving Hope an outer appearance of a completely different person. Long red hair fell in straight rivers around her form and the dress she wore was dark against pure porcelain skin, almost having a statuesque quality to it.

"You look perfect." Meg spoke, nodding. "It won't fool him for long, but we just need to distract him for long enough to get Da Vinci to the altar where the Libro Sacro sits. You will not be alone; we will be behind you the whole time."

"What if he catches on. How do we get out if something goes wrong?" Hope was running through scenarios in her head, while Leonardo simply stood by listening and thinking. His left arm rested across his chest, his right hand holding his index finger to his lips, seeming very distracted at the moment and lost in his own thoughts. After Hope's question the quiet Aēshma stepped forward, pulling a long-wrapped item from a long case she had held on her back. She unwrapped the item and offered it to Hope. The item was the shiniest, silver sword Hope had ever seen. Intricate designs not only lined the metal, but the hilt and handle as well. Purple colored leather straps dangled from the handle, which Hope assumed were to keep a good grip of the sword. The designs on the sword seemed varied, like the sword had been made specifically for Hope, as she recognized both the symbols and imagery of Heaven and Hell as if it were telling a story upon it. It looked heavy, but as the woman handed the weapon to her, Hope almost lost her balance because of how light it actually was. She'd never experienced anything like it, it was light as a feather and as her hand grasped the handle, the symbols lit up bright in their respective red and blue auras, a mixture of energies which again created the purplish hue surrounding the blade. Hope stared at it, admiring the weapon. As she did so, the large woman wrapped Hope's chest in a delicate leather sheath, it was also decorated and seemed to fit like a glove around Hope, to allow her to carry the weapon on her back. "Thank you." Hope spoke to Aēshma, simply receiving a nod from the woman, however she had still yet to utter a single word.

"It is beautiful, isn't it?" Meg said, smiling as she referred to the sword. "Magnesium-Carbon, Damascus Steel. The lightest, strongest, longest lasting and most spiritually malleable metal in…" She paused, gesturing to her surroundings. "…well, all of the worlds. A weapon of which can only be forged in the waters of the Stagnum Ignis ." She looked over at Leonardo, who had barely moved the whole time, seeming to be figuring something in his head and using his fingers in front of him to manipulate something that only he could see. "We have one for you too, sugar lips." The comment made Hope blush and wonder if she knew what had happened in Veranon's illusion, but then she let it go as it didn't really matter and it wasn't any of the woman's business, anyway. As Aēshma began to fit Leo with his harness, he was caught from his thoughts and back to reality.

"Oh. Thank you." Leonardo was grateful for the gift, but it didn't seem to be as important to him as it was to their allies. Hope knew what he was doing, even if the others did not. Leonardo was distracted, because in his mind he was running through probabilities and possible scenarios of how this plan would play out. Though he didn't have all of the variables, he seemed to be accounting for those variables so that they would be prepared for almost anything. After a mere few minutes more, Leonardo haphazardly put the sword given to him in the sheath without actually inspecting it, he seemed to wrap up his thought processes and bring his focus back to what was going on in the current. "Let's go."

"What is your hurry, Architect?" Meg smiled, something about her smile was odd, but Hope dismissed it as nothing major. It was possible that the Fury was nervous about the plan or maybe she just wasn't in a rush to commit treason against her home. The girl could understand why she might delay the situation, but she also knew Da Vinci was on a time limit. She knew he was likely getting close to the end of the effectiveness of what Deus had given him and the Knight had reminded him to keep track of his limits. She wasn't sure what might happen, but it likely wasn't good. She could only assume the obvious, that without the demonic tint to his human soul, they could be seen by others ahead of achieving their goal.

"Not all of us have an eternity to procrastinate." Leo's answer was simple, but it was obvious that her question seemed odd to him, as well. He, like Hope, let the comment go. Though he remained more on guard after her odd behavior.

"Very well." Meg began to lead the group out of Vera's door and back into the decorated hallway. However, instead of moving away, she simply closed the door behind them. She then faced it again. Lifting her hand, she used a small blade to slice her palm, then placed it to Vera's door. Her blood was black, not red, and she drew a symbol that Hope had never seen before inside of her bloody palm print. "Firmamentum est ad Inferos ." Veranon didn't seem to like that Meg was doing this to her door, by the look on her face, but didn't say anything.

When Meg once again opened the door using the pressure plate, it was no longer Vera's room. Instead, it revealed a medieval style library. The walls held many wooden shelves and on them were more books than Hope had ever seen before. The ceilings were so high that she almost couldn't see them. There were items in cases here and there, but she didn't see any guard yet. For that matter, she didn't see anyone. Veranon and Aēshma stayed back by the door, but Leonardo and Hope followed Meg, as per the plan. They made their way through the library and Hope inspected each part of the room as they walked through, wishing she had time to see everything in more detail. Suddenly, Meg stopped and quietly motioned to Da Vinci to take a different direction. He did as she said quickly, as Meg and Hope moved further through the library. It wasn't long before Hope saw a large opening, in front of which stood a young man.

His appearance seemed that of a seventeen- or eighteen-year-old boy, but he certainly wasn't completely normal looking. His tousled hair was a bright red-orange, a color Hope hadn't ever seen a human naturally have. The skin around his eyes was very dark almost as if he were wearing gothic make-up, accentuated by his porcelain, white skin, though the color of his eyes was a jarring, brilliant emerald. He had a slim, yet muscular frame, seeming normal for fit a young man. He didn't look particularly intimidating, though the confidence that he exuded was almost startling. He stood with his arms crossing his chest, in front of the door frame, almost like a statue. His clothing was a bit dated, but not in any way extravagant or notable. He wore a loose white shirt, seeming to have come from the renaissance era, as did his plain brown pants both seeming to have been made for a much larger individual. He did not wear shoes, his bare feet stood on the red carpet that had led the three through the library toward the sacred room. She could barely see past the young man, but there was something extremely powerful in the room he guarded. Even without using her vision, she could see that the whole room pulsed and radiated energy. When the two women caught the young man's attention, he seemed taken off guard for a moment."

"Navar?" The man's voice was a bit lower than Hope had expected it to be and in order to inspect the women, he moved out of the doorway and toward them. As he walked, his steps seemed heavier than they should have been, something about him was off. Hope didn't dare use her vision, she didn't want the man to see through the illusion, at least not yet.

"Lord Yue Malik, we have come to speak to you..." As Megaera spoke, Da Vinci quietly moved behind the guard, and disappeared into the room. "I know you weren't expecting us and, to be honest, I wasn't expecting to be here either." Hope wasn't sure where Meg was going with this, but it seemed like she was stalling, surely the man would know what she was doing. The minutes seemed to pass by so slowly that Hope began to feel uncomfortable.

"Silence." Admon seemed to have no interest in Meg's long-winded explanation. "Child, why are you here?" He directed the question toward Hope and caused a pit to begin growing in her stomach. She didn't know what to say and so she just stared at him, a blank expression on her face.

"Now, now Admon. Let's not be impatient." Meg seemed indifferent toward the man and, in that moment, something about her seemed to change. "Is that how you treat some-one who comes baring gifts?" Hope's instincts began to tell her that 'the plan' was about to go very wrong. However, for now, it was simply suspicion. She could have been speaking of bringing his daughter to him as a gift, however as she con-tinued, all doubt was removed, and the plan quickly began to fall apart. "Admon Yue Malik, meet Hope...she is the newest Talyâ d'Alâhâ...and a chimera, at that." Meg began to step back as she watched the anger grow in the young man's eyes. Hope expected his aura to grow and magic levels to rise, but what actually happened caught her completely by surprise.

The ripping sound of cloth began to echo through the high walls of the vault, as the lower half of his body began to expand until the fabric of his clothing ripped to pieces and fell to the floor. Unfolding from the human form, an extremely dark red exoskeleton began to fill the area within the doorframe. The top half of him remained human, but the bottom half was slowly shifting into a creature unlike she'd ever seen before. Behind him, a dagger-like stinger, at the end of a long, armor plated tail, rose above his head. It seemed as if it could easily impale her with one swift move-ment. She now could see why he guarded the book. She had heard of centaurs, half human and half man. However, never in her life had she heard of a creature that was half human and half scorpion. The scorpion lower half of his body was three times as large as his human-like legs had been, Hope was momentarily confused as to exactly how it had even been possible to compact the massive body into the small limbs, by comparison, that he'd had before. Though she didn't have much time to ponder, as he took on a defensive stance, ready to fight the outsider.

"How dare you trespass on sacred ground and imperson-ate my child in order to deceive me." His tail hovered behind him, almost like he was itching to strike at the girl. "You will not be leaving here in the same way that you came." Hope let the illusion drop and the appearance of Navar faded, as she pulled out the sword that she'd been given. She wasn't completely sure that she trusted it, as she had already been betrayed once. It was hard to know if any of them had been sincere about their assistance. Hope held the, now glowing, sword at the ready, having no idea how to use it. She sup-posed that one would just aim and swing. She glanced toward where Meg had been, and the woman was now nowhere to be found. Hope was alone and massive amounts of adrenaline being pumped through her body made her want to throw up. She hoped Da Vinci hurried.

"We don't want to take anything; we just want to read the book." Hope tried to reason with him. She didn't understand why it was so forbidden to be near it. It wasn't like they could grab a book containing the entire history of time itself and take off with it. Hope still wasn't sure exactly how Da Vinci planned on reading it in such a short amount of time anyway. She didn't have much time to contemplate it, as Admon thrust the stinger toward her. She dodged the attack, but the strike had been a bit too close for comfort. She swung the sword at him and while it did hit the creature, the metal bounced off of the rock-hard exoskeleton of the creature. She blinked once. She had to rethink her plan of action. She would likely need to use the sword on the fleshy human half of him, as it seemed that she would not be getting through the scorpion body. Within the split second that Hope regrouped, Admon lashed his tail out to sweep beneath her, while also reaching out to grab her with one of the two large pincers that had, up until that point, hovered in front of his body in an attack ready position. Hope dodged the claw, but as the creature's tail lashed out, she was unable to move out of the way fast enough. The impact of the appendage slammed against her body like someone had hit her with a small wrecking ball and tossed her across the room. Admon followed to where she had landed, to attack while she was down, which had left the doorway unguarded. The blow had knocked the wind out of the girl, and she gasped to regain her bearings. It hurt to breathe, and she watched helplessly as the creature moved toward her. As massive as his body was, the weight made his crawling movements slow, unlike the lithe movements the human form had suggested. Hope knew she was outmatched and became afraid, beginning to accept that they had already failed, and they weren't getting out of here alive. They had known it was a long shot, this was going to be how her story would end.

It was in that moment; something caused the tides to begin to turn. Seemingly out of nowhere, something invisible hit Yue Malik, not only catching him off guard, but Hope watched as jagged claw marks sliced down the creature's human torso. Admon's arm thrust through the air connecting with the invisible threat and Hope heard a loud yelp. It had been the tiny Hellhound, protecting his chosen owner. She was sure the pup wasn't thinking of his own safety when he attacked the other creature, his only concern had been help-ing her. She hoped he was okay, but she didn't have time to think about that for the moment, she needed to get to her feet and fight for both of their sakes. Through the deep scratches, Hope could see something that almost caused her to have a panic attack. Beneath the scratches there was not tender flesh and organs. Under the humanoid skin, the exoskeleton continued, as an endoskeleton. She couldn't breathe, the air seemed to get thinner, and Hope began to hyperventilate. He couldn't be injured, there was no way she would be able to pierce the rock hard, natural armor. There was now not any question in her mind as to why he had been chosen to guard the book, the man was basically indestructible.

Just when she had again accepted her fate, she was grabbed by the arm and pulled away from the situation. She heard a loud whistle and the scrapping of animal nails against the floor. Leonardo shoved Hope through a portal he had created on the wall while Admon had been distracted by the Hell pup. When he was sure they were all three through the portal, he took the blade he had been given and slashed through the sigil, closing the portal. Admon was not fast enough to follow, but now they had been exposed. It was just a matter of time before they were found and caught by whoever might have been paying attention. Leo hurried, helping Hope to her feet.

"How did you do that? If you can do that, why did we need Asmodeus to do it for us?" Hope was confused. She could hear the young pup panting, so she knew he was alright, satisfying her concern for him.

"I can create connections from one room to another, but dimensional gateways are beyond my capabilities at this time." He looked both ways, before moving to an empty wall and beginning to draw another symbol. When it lit up, activated, he once again grabbed her and forced her to jump through. He seemed to have a specific destination in mind this time, unlike the last time when he was simply trying to get away from the immediate threat. Once through and the location faded into view, Hope shifted her gaze back and forth from Leo to the landscape in front of her.

"No. Absolutely not, I'm not doing that." Hope shook her head stubbornly.

"You would rather stay here and have another conversation with Yue Malik?" Leo asked the rhetorical question moving toward a small boat where an individual was waiting. The boat, however, did not sit on water. In fact, it was what it *did* sit on that caused Hope to protest so strongly to begin with. The boat floated on a lake of lava. A *literal* lake of molten lava. She had thought it was a figure of speech or a cautionary tale, she wouldn't have ever imagined that the theological lake was so literal. Around the edges of the seemingly wooden gondola, tiny flashes of fire rose up like waves, putting the proverbial cherry on top of the situation. Leonardo began to speak to the ferryman and, without touching the individual, Da Vinci gave him three large gold coins. Leo motioned for Hope to come along, getting into the boat himself, and as the pup hopped into the boat, it rocked upon the lava causing even more fiery bursts around the small vessel. Hope stepped into the boat carefully and sat down. Once seated, she looked toward the boat's captain.

It was a man, in a black cloak and as the boat began to move, the man remained completely still, he simply stared at Hope. She could tell that he was thin beneath his attire, so thin that his face was gaunt, and one could almost see every bone in his body structure, even though the draping attire. A small amount of sparse, dark hair rested on his forehead beneath his hood. It didn't take long before Hope realized exactly who this individual was, the thought of which was far from comforting. She turned toward Leo and whispered to him, of which came out much louder than she had intended it to be.

"You got an Uber from *Death*?!" She seemed both shocked and terrified.

"He's neutral. He was on the list." Leo spoke nonchalantly.

"Oh yeah, sure...because the list worked out so well before." With every word he spoke, Hope became angrier at him.

"You realize, I am not deaf." The voice came from across the boat, as he directed his comment to both of them. However, his next comment was directed only toward Da Vinci. "When you are once again in your world, you're going to want to do something about that." He didn't specify what he was talking about, but he nodded toward Hope. A confused look crossed the faces of both humans, until a scratch on Hope's arm caught their eyes. It wasn't deep or even bleeding very much, but it had begun to spread a black substance through her veins around the wound. Having had so much adrenaline pumping through her body, she hadn't even realized that she had gotten scratched at all. Let alone apparently hit by the venomous stinger. Almost as soon as she had seen it, the dark veins began burning as if they were pushing acid through her bloodstream. By the time they reached the other side of the lake, Hope had collapsed and fell unconscious, her body slowly beginning to be overcome by the poison. Leo carried her out of the boat and onto the shore, near what he assumed to be the gate. Once they went through the decorated entry, they would be home, but he was unsure if he could even take her back to their own world yet. He didn't know what might happen if they crossed back into their own world with the foreign substance still in her body. Would the spread be worse? Would she survive the crossing? Would the black substance go away? The Architect was not one to take that kind of chance.

Laying there on the bank of the Lake of Fire, Hope woke up long enough to vomit a liquid like a thick, black tar. Her body was beginning to reject the foreign substance within her system, but the hostile takeover of her body grew stronger, much faster than her body could reject it. It burned unlike anything she had ever felt before and the smell of her vomit was so overwhelmingly sulfuric that it was almost too much to bear. Leo was noticeably concerned, which Hope knew meant that the situation was *very* bad. The man rarely allowed his emotions to be seen and generally remained calm. Currently, he seemed almost panicked.

"I am going to go get help. I will be back soon." He looked up and around, not knowing where the young dog was, but speaking to it anyway. "Stay with her. Protect her." With that, the man ran to the gate and disappeared as he jumped through with reckless disregard. It was getting harder for Hope to breathe, especially considering she was sure when Admon had knocked the wind out of her he had likely broken a rib. Though her ribs were the least of her concerns, whereas the toxin was beginning to quickly affect every part of her body. After a few moments, she fell back into unconsciousness.

Lexicon of the Chronicler

[Note: I am not fluent in any of these languages (except for English) and I would ask you to take into consideration that the way definitions are worded is not my own style of doing things. I used online translators for anything that I couldn't handle myself. I created this glossary because personally, when I read, I don't like the flow of my reading to be interrupted and thought that there might be others out there that share my opinion. I want my readers to understand my books, but at the same time, I don't like interrupting the story.]

Talyâ d'Alâhâ [Galilean Aramaic] - Child of God

'Almah [Hebrew] - Young Woman

Bonum mane, Deifilia [Latin] - Good morning, God's daughter.

Deifilia [Latin] - Daughter of God

Dei Malleo [Latin] - Hammer of God

Elenin [Hebrew] - Hammer of God

Deus his opus habet videre in mane coram. Vocationem Yhidrial hoc est, non velle puer per Deum. [Latin] - Deus needs to see you before morning. You should call Yhidrial this does not concern the Child of God.

Puer Deus [Latin] - Child of God

Caelum et Infernum [Latin] - Heaven and Hell

Beannachtaí. An bhfuil tú réidh, leanbh Dé [Gaelic] - Greetings, are you ready to go, Child of God.

Tá [Gaelic] - Yes.

M'ainm is Venetia [Gaelic] My name is Venetia.

Venetia [Gaelic] - Blessed

Slán, ba bhreá liom bualadh leat [Gaelic] - Goodbye, It was a pleasure to meet you.

Tum'ah Dām [Hebrew] - Impure Blood, Monsters, Creatures, Outsiders

Carissimi unum [Latin] - Dear One

Ytzr kshr [Hebrew] - Contact

Hiys'tor'yah, Dvry Ymy Hvr [Hebrew] - Heaven's Bible, the History of Time Itself in its entirety, as recorded by Heaven.

Libro Sacro or *In Libro Inferos* - [Latin] Hell's Bible, Sacred Book, the Book of Hell, according to Hell's perspective of time.

Filia Dei [Latin] - Daughter of God

Dulcedo [Latin] - Sweetness

Quid tu hic agis? [Latin] - What are you doing here?

Nos sunt hic ad armata Megaera quaedam de opinione

citius intercepti. [Latin] - We are here to see Megaera concerning some urgent business.

Sequere [Latin] - Follow

Ut ostium crinem solvere ingredi [Latin] - Loosen the lock of this door, so I may enter.

Megaera veniam sunt externis theatrum petens [Latin] - Beg pardon Megaera, there are outsiders requesting an audience.

Firmamentum est ad Inferos [Latin] - The Vault of Hell

Sanctus Mater [Latin] - Holy Mother

Vorago [Latin] - The abyss; the name for Hell, before it became Hell.

Stagnum Ignis [Latin] - Lake of Fire

AMW Volume
One: The End is
the Beginning is
the End
First Publication Date:
April 7th, 2021

AMW Volume Two:
Once Upon a Time
In Detroit...
ETA: Undetermined

Visit the Archives of Metaphysical Warfare on the web at:
https://www.archivesofmetaphysicalwarfare.com/
and
https://www.facebook.com/archivesofmetaphysicalwarfare

Join the fight with merch for your chosen allies!

About the Chronicler

[This section was written by some of the most important people in my life. I can write about a million imaginary characters, but I have a terrible time figuring out what to write about myself. So, in the interest of such, I decided to allow you all to see who I am from the perspective of some of the individuals in my life who know me the best. These are copied word for word, as they gave them to me. Pardon any errors, they are not professional writers. These are their raw words.]

My daughter Charity has went through many life changing experiences, much more than the average person could or would want to handle. She has come out as a stronger woman, ready always to tackle the next hurdle that comes along. She is a mother who would go to the end protecting her children and helping them through their daily struggles. She is strong in her faith and it has helped her through so much. I have always been amazed at her artistic abilities whether they be as an artist with a brush or as a writer. I'm looking forward to reading her book and the adventures she puts before me. I'm sure she will put a lot of herself deep into its characters and their adventures.

• Debbie C. (Mother)

Charity could have been a scientist of anything, but chose to be happy & have the life she has today.

• Jim W. (Father)

My sister is someone you listen to. Someone to listen to about advice, knowledge, and stories whether they are true or made up.

Charity, has this creative mind that could always take us on adventures. Showing me how to fish in puddles and make mud pies growing up on our farm as kids. But while our childhood years were fun and they went by too quickly, Charity also had to grow up quick. Having two beautiful and kind children, my niece and nephew, shortly after high school. Along the way, she attended college and worked following a passion for art as she always had a pen to paper.

We couldn't be more happy and proud of her to bring this

passion to a reality with her first book! Love you so much, Chelsey Jojo.

• Chelsey A. (Sister)

Charity is the most caring person I know. I'm incredibly proud of how much work, time, and energy she has spent on this book. She truly has a gift when it comes to creativity and the ability to convey her message in writing. I'm very blessed to be her husband.

• Jeremey Gaff (Husband)

My mom is one of the most kind hearted people you'll ever meet. Quite honestly, she's my hero. She is always so hard working. She loves writing. It gets her out of her own head and into someone else's. She's so creative with it. I am so proud of her for how far she's gotten and become. She's her own person. This book is a part of her though. A part of her that she hasn't allowed anyone to really see until now. I believe she will go far.

• Faith (Daughter)

www.ingramcontent.com/pod-product-compliance
Lightning Source LLC
Chambersburg PA
CBHW070646100726
47907CB00007B/2114